SHADY BORDERS

Recent Titles by John Sherwood

SHADY BORDERS

John Sherwood

This first world edition published in Great Britain 1996 by
SEVERN HOUSE PUBLISHERS LTD of
9–15 High Street, Sutton, Surrey SM1 1DF.
First published in the USA 1996 by
SEVERN HOUSE PUBLISHERS INC. of
595 Madison Avenue, New York, NY 10022.

British Library Cataloguing in Publication Data

Sherwood, John, 1913–
    Shady borders
    1. English fiction – 20th century
    I. Title
    823.9'14 [F]

    ISBN 0-7278-5111-X

Typeset by Palimpsest Book Production Limited,
Polmont, Stirlingshire, Scotland.
Printed and bound in Great Britain by
Hartnolls Ltd, Bodmin, Cornwall.

Chapter One

Horrors, thought Celia Grant as the house came into view. It was a formidable outburst of eighteenth century one-upmanship plonked down in the peaceful Hampshire countryside. Its grand central block, topped by a dome, had a broad flight of steps leading up to an entrance portico guarded by a roof-high array of pillars. Nothing had been skimped in the wings stretching away on either side, and the park contained all the proper status symbols: a lake, an assortment of little temples, a fake ruin and the usual clumps of trees tastefully dotted about.

Winthrop Court had been been built to house a large family, plus dozens of guests, a small army of servants, and any number of miscellaneous hangers-on. Two and a half centuries later its survival presented its owner with a massive financial headache, which was being dealt with by the method usual in such cases. The entrance charges, displayed on a notice board by the pair of entrance lodges, had struck Celia as fairly stiff.

When she told her Uncle Hugo that she had been summoned to Winthrop, he provided her with some background. "I haven't seen Charley Clandon for years. He used to be a dull old thing, working for various boring good causes and making gloomy speeches in the House of Lords about the nation's morals. But that's all changed now, I'm told."

"Why? What's happened?"

"He's got a sprightly new wife, half his age, and she's galvanised him into activity. They're turning the place into

1

a tourist attraction. I suppose they want you to help them pretty the garden up."

"Fine, but if I work for them will they pay my bill?"

"Oh yes. His grandfather married an American corn-flake heiress."

"But you know what the aristocracy are like. The richer they are, the longer they take to pay up."

"Remember, he used to be a Holy Joe, a very stiff pillar of the Church. And as I say, he's very well-heeled."

Privately Celia was not optimistic. Archerscroft Nurseries was prospering, but could not afford to write off bad debts, and she hated the unpleasantness of dunning people for money.

Up at the house there were notices everywhere directing the sightseers to the toilets, the restaurant, the children's playground and the gardens. The large car park provided for the paying customers' benefit was almost full. As instructed, Celia ignored it and drove into the stable yard beside the house, which was used as a staff car park.

A service entrance to the house opened on to the yard. Inside, in the echoing cellars, was a cafeteria in which early arrivals were already having morning coffee. She had been told to ask there for the entrance to the private wing inhabited by the family, and was directed by one of the waitresses to a stone staircase which led up to the ground floor. At the top was a door with a letterbox and a bell, which she rang.

A pleasant looking middle-aged woman in an apron let her in. "Mrs Grant? His Lordship is expecting you, he's in the business room. This way, please."

A corridor, replete with mahogany doors in decorative cases contrasted with the austere kitchen quarters below.

The 'business room' (which in a less aristocratic commercial enterprise would have been called the office) lay at the end of the corridor. Its door was open. Lord Clandon was standing by an old-fashioned roll-top desk on the far side of the room. Facing him was a man with pale, cold eyes behind rimless spectacles, who was holding the door handle as if on his way out. Celia waited outside for him to finish his business and leave, but no one moved and nothing seemed to be happening. It was clear, though, that whatever had just happened had been dramatic, and had left the two furious with each other. The man by the door was red with anger to the roots of his mousy hair, and his hand on the door knob was trembling. Lord Clandon was glaring at him from across the room like the angel expelling Adam and Eve.

"Mrs Grant is here, my lord," ventured the house-keeper.

The tense tableau unfroze. "Ah, Mrs Grant, thank you for coming," said Lord Clandon. "This is our estate manager, George Glenville."

Without speaking, Glenville gave Celia a hot damp hand which was stiff with anger.

"Then that's settled, George," said Clandon, dismissing him.

"Yes, I suppose so," hissed Glenville furiously and went, leaving Celia to take stock of Charles Augustus Winthrop, Fourteenth Earl of Clandon. He was in his sixties, tall and thin, with hawklike features, and the suppressed energies of a man determined to get on with things and not settle down to growing old. But as he greeted her his smile did not spread to his eyes from the grim lines round his mouth. The aura of gloom described by Sir Hugo still clung to him.

He gestured apologetically at the desk and filing cabinets. "Let's go and talk somewhere more comfortable, and you must meet my wife."

They found her in the family sitting-room, further along the corridor on the garden side of the house. She was rather a surprise. The features in her round face were undistinguished and her figure dumpy, and although her honey-blonde hair and hazel eyes could be considered assets, she did not by any means qualify as a much older

3

man's tempting bit of fluff. If she was 'sprightly' this had yet to appear.

The housekeeper brought mid-morning coffee. Over it the subject of the garden was not mentioned and Celia, gazing out through french windows on to a terrace overlooking a well-kept lawn, wondered when it would be. But there seemed to be a hidden agenda. Lady Clandon kept glancing unobtrusively at her watch, and seemed to be making some silent appeal to her husband. Presently she said: "Charles, have you noticed the time?"

"Oh. Yes Harriet, thank you for reminding me. We'll talk about the garden later, Mrs Grant, but would you mind doing us a great favour first?"

Celia wondered uneasily what was coming.

"You came in through the private entrance from the stable yard, is that right?" he asked.

"Yes."

"Good. So none of the paying customers saw you. The point is, a guided tour of the house is about to begin. Would you mind awfully joining the tour and telling us afterwards if you notice anything odd?"

"Please do," begged Lady Clandon. "I know it's horribly bad form of us to exploit you. But there's a squalid nuisance that's been plaguing us for some time, and I'd happily sell my grandmother for cat's meat to get rid of it."

Celia's hackles rose. She was sick of people who tried to inveigle her into solving little mysteries for them on the basis of her reputation as an amateur detective; it was as bad as discussing one's symptoms with a doctor one met at a party. Had these privileged lordlings summoned her because someone was stealing the spoons, with no real intention of employing her in their garden?

"Wouldn't it be better if you employed a private detective?" she said coldly.

"No no, my dear Mrs Grant, it's not that sort of problem; any responsible and intelligent person would

4

do, provided they're not known to be connected with the management here."

She was mollified. Unless he was lying in his teeth, he knew nothing of her hectic career as a latter-day Miss Marple. It would be churlish to refuse.

"Thank you," said Lord Clandon when she accepted. "We must hurry, though, the tour will be starting any moment now."

Without further explanation he bustled her back down the basement stairs and out into the stable yard. "If you wouldn't mind going round to the main entrance . . . Here's some money for the entrance fee, so that they think you're just an ordinary member of the public."

Wondering crossly what oddities she was supposed to look out for, Celia skirted round the house and climbed the steps to the grand entrance. Having paid for her ticket she joined the motley group of sightseers waiting under the dome of the vast central hall for the tour of the house to begin.

Their guide was a tall, well-built man in his forties with a military moustache and a sergeant major's voice. In a muted bellow he glossed hastily over the early history of the Winthrop family and announced that the Fourth Earl had knocked down a ramshackle Tudor house in the seventeen thirties and built "this magnificent mansion". Celia wondered how the Winthrops had amassed the money needed to build it. Dragging helpless heiresses to the altar? Currying favour with royalty? Corrupt holders of public office had limitless opportunities for plunder.

Winthrop, the guide explained, was at last coming into its own again after a long period of decline and neglect. For over twenty years it had been let to a community of Anglican nuns, and His Lordship had lived in a small farmhouse on the estate. But after his marriage to Her Ladyship, he had decided to reopen the house as a family home, restore it to its former glory and allow its treasures to be enjoyed by a wider public. None of this would have been possible without the enthusiasm, hard work and sure taste of Her Ladyship, who was largely reponsible for the marvels which the tour was about to see.

Keeping her eyes open for oddities, she followed the group into a splendid drawing room with red silk walls, and a carpet on the floor which echoed the pattern of the elaborate plasterwork on the ceiling. The guide explained that the ceiling was by Robert Adam, enriched with medallions by Angelica Kaufmann, and that the silk walls and specially woven carpet were recent additions for which the impeccable taste of Her Ladyship was responsible. This, he added, was one of many instances of her valuable help in the restoration of the house.

Celia reflected that the valuable help could not have included a significant infusion of money. According to Sir Hugo, Charley Clandon had married his secretary. So how had all this refurbishment been paid for? It must have cost the earth. According to Sir Hugo, the breakfast food heiress had left the family well off; very well off, if its finances could stand expenditure on this scale.

Next, the guide led his charges into a long corridor lined on both sides with a collection of fine porcelain, mostly early Chelsea and Bow. Celia shrank away from the rows of simpering shepherdesses and mythological ladies. Her white hair, fresh complexion and tiny, trim figure made her look uncomfortably like one of them herself.

After touching briefly on a complete monkey orchestra by Kändler from Meissen, the guide drew special attention to the fine workmanship of the glass cases displaying the collection. They had been designed, he said, by Her Ladyship herself.

It soon dawned on Celia that the oddity she was supposed to take notice of was the loud-voiced guide himself. In the music room and library that followed he dwelt ecstatically on Her Ladyship's choice of curtain materials and soft furnishings, which received more wordage than pictures by Gainsborough and Reynolds, console tables by Sheraton and a desk by William Vile. She was also responsible, it seemed, for the flower arrangements, which struck Celia as competent without being outstanding.

The guide's awed fixation on Her Ladyship had also been noticed by others. "He's got the hots for her, I reckon," muttered a spotty youth with earrings.

"Horny old bugger," agreed his girlfriend. Murmurs and nervous laughter from the group confirmed that others shared their opinion.

On one side of the marble fireplace hung a portrait of Lord Clandon, staring out grimly from the canvas in a dark suit.

"Sour-looking old bastard, ain't he?" muttered the youth with earrings. "Maybe Her Ladyship's got a thing going with lover-boy here."

"I would if I was her," agreed his girlfriend. "With a beefy voice like that, lover-boy would have nice big balls, wouldn't he? Old misery there looks as if his are tiny."

On the other side of the fireplace hung a companion picture representing a dark-haired, dark-eyed young woman who was either beautiful or had been made to seem so by the skill of a fashionable portrait painter. An elderly lady in the group asked if it represented Lady Clandon.

The guide eyed the questioner severely. "No, madam. That portrait by De Lazlo is of His Lordship's first wife. Eighteen years had to pass before he found happiness with Her Ladyship."

"Oh dear," lamented the elderly lady. "Was his first marriage dreadfully unhappy?"

"I have no information about that, madam."

During Celia's briefing by Sir Hugo, she had asked if there had been a divorce.

"Good heavens no, Charley was much too proper, and they were perfectly happy as far as I know. They had two daughters and she died while producing the second one. Then there was this long gap, after which to everyone's surprise wife number two upped and provided him with a son and heir."

"Why were you all surprised, Uncle Hugo?"

"Because by then he was over sixty. A lot of cynical eyebrows were raised. But I'm sure the child was his. Anything else would have been unthinkable in a man of his character."

The last of the state rooms on the ground floor was a dining room, with the long table laid out for the tourists' benefit with superb china and glass as if for a grand dinner party. In the very middle was a silver-gilt centre-piece, a stupendous object almost two feet tall, elaborately decorated in the rococo manner with flowers and fruit and shells. It was topped by a male and a female nude embracing in a manner too languid to be really provocative.

"In the centre of the table," bellowed the guide, "is the Augsburg table centre, so called because it was created in eighteen-forty by the great gold and silversmith Christian Ludkens of Augsburg. It has been valued at over fifteen million pounds, and was a gift from the Empress Catherine the Great of Russia to the Sixth Earl when he was ambassador in Saint Petersburg. The figures on the top represent the goddess Venus and a beautiful human youth called Adonis, with whom she had a love affair." He winked suggestively. "The Empress Catherine was a very amorous woman, who gave magnificent gifts to her lovers."

After the silver-gilt monstrosity had been gaped at sufficiently, the tour continued upstairs, where a range of bedrooms had been fitted up for display rather than sleep, with the magic touch of Her Ladyship manifested in an excessive yardage of frills. The tourists were then taken down to the basement to marvel at the inconveniences of the unused and unusable Victorian kitchen. They were then expelled into a souvenir shop which smelt oppressively of herbs, and through it out of the service entrance.

But Celia had to report her findings about the lovesick guide to the Clandons. The guide was on his way out of the building, and as she headed towards the stone stairs leading to the private wing on the ground floor, he recognised her as a member of his group. "So you're another of their bloody spies, are you?" he growled and stood staring after her as she vanished round the corner of the stairs.

Back with the couple in their sitting room, she described what she had observed, and added that the guide's obvious admiration of Lady Clandon had given rise to a certain amount of ribaldry.

"Ribaldry?" the earl asked with grim determination not to be amused.

"Jokey speculation about a possible relationship between him and your wife," Celia explained cagily.

"There, Charles, you see?" said Lady Clandon. "I kept telling you, Peter Harding must go."

"Of course, my dear Harriet. But we had to have evidence first from at least two witnesses, and now we've got it. He can't take proceedings against us for wrongful dismissal."

Celia was furious at being trapped. Now she would have to give evidence if needed at an industrial tribunal. And there was still no guarantee of a profitable gardening contract.

"Harding will be back this afternoon to take the three o'clock tour," said Harriet Chandon. "Will you speak to him after that?"

"Certainly, my dear. But now we have traded on Mrs Grant's kindness for long enough. I must show her the garden and get down to business with her."

"Thank you," said Celia drily. "I would like that."

"Let's go out this way, then."

He led her out of the french windows on to the terrace. During her tour she had spied out the land through the windows of the public rooms, and established that the

9

lawn beyond the terrace was flanked by mixed borders against a background of old-established trees. Her spirits rose. If this was all the garden consisted of so far, there were hopes after all of lucrative business.

"When the nuns had the place they kept things fairly tidy up here," Clandon explained. "But it was all they could manage. Everything down below was a frighful mess after all those years of neglect, but the bare bones of the garden were still there, once I'd got it cleared."

Advancing to the end of the lawn, Celia saw her hopes dashed. An elaborate pattern of walks and flowerbeds had already been laid out on the south-facing slope below. Clearly the restoration of the garden had proceeded with the same energy and disregard for expense as the refurbishment of the house. Before her a long grass walk between two herbaceous borders led down to a lawn at the bottom, with a stone balustrade overhanging the river. On the far bank, parkland sloped up to a belt of trees.

In front of where she stood a wide path ran across the garden at right angles to the slope, with statues ranged along it at regular intervals. Before leaving the house Clandon had given her a brochure containing a plan of the garden. She consulted it. "You call this 'Lady Betty's walk'."

"Yes, after my dear old aunt, Betty Fitzwarren. Her memory still haunts it."

He fixed Celia with a vaguely uncomfortable stare, as if his conscience made telling lies uncomfortable. Celia had a sudden intuition that the walk had been named to pander to the sentimentality of the tourists, and that the real Lady Betty was a foul-mouthed hard-drinking foxhunter who scarely knew a daffodil from an orchid.

The borders on either side of the long downhill vista were fully planted and already showing a little early summer colour. So far she could see nothing for her to do. But instead of starting off down it, Clandon led the way to one side along the cross-walk. At the end was a

10

pool, romantically backed by sheltering trees. "Helena's pool," he murmured, looking uncomfortable again. "After my mother."

From the pool he led the way downhill through a series of specialised enclosures; a white garden, a large rose garden, a spring walk which was already over, separate pergolas for wisteria, laburnum and rambler roses, and gardens designed to be at their best at various seasons of the year. Some of the planting was very recent, but had been done knowledgeably and with taste. His enthusiasm for horticulture might be a recent development born of the need to make Winthrop financially viable, but he had taken the job seriously. Again the problem arose. What, if anything, had he left a professional garden designer to do?

They had reached the river bank at the bottom of the slope. But instead of heading back towards the house up the central grass path between the long borders, he crossed it to the far side. In front of them a small stone building was half hidden in overgrown woodland. "The Temple of Flora," he announced. But as it had been named by the ancestor who built it, there was no need this time for him to look uncomfortable.

The next feature to be inspected was a group of beds devoted to varieties of the genus cornus.

"I collect them," he told her. "One of my prides and joys. They grow very well here in this sandy loam, with the canopy of trees overhead to give light shade. In fact I've written to ask if I can hold the National Cornus Collection* here."

---

*The National Collections are assembled to bring together as many cultivars as possible of a given genus, to ensure that none of them become extinct. Many of the collections are held by amateurs, in private gardens large and small. But Celia was right. Permission to hold the National Collection of Cornus had already been applied for successfully by Mr and Mrs Compton of Newby Hall in Yorkshire.

Celia obliged by taking a proper interest in the cornuses. There were twenty or thirty species in the beds, all named on cast-iron name-tags stuck in the ground beside them. But she was no nearer knowing what she was wanted for, and remembered vaguely that there was already a National Cornus Collection somewhere else.

"Now," said Clandon to her surprise and relief. "Let me show you the problem I'd like you to solve."

He took her back into the central vista and they advanced up the grass walk. The borders to either side, presumably the first area to be planted, would soon be a riot of colour. At the top of the walk a flight of stone steps confronted them, so steep that it was impossible to see what lay above. Climbing them, Celia found nothing but a semicircular area of grass.

"You see?" said Clandon. "This should be the climax of the whole composition, the ultimate experience as the visitor ends his tour of the garden. And what is there here? Anti-climax. Nothing."

Celia did not think the anti-climax deplorable. It seemed to her that a restful area of well-kept grass would be a welcome relief after the expanses of hectic colour below. But it would clearly be tactless to say so.

"I have been cudgelling my brains about this all winter without a solution. Do please have some ideas, Mrs Grant."

Horrors, Celia thought. After what the tourists would have seen already, massive overkill would be needed to provide an ultimate experience rather than a damp squib. She looked at the site again. It was semicircular, bounded by the curved retaining wall of the level above. Topiary would be sensible, to provide relief after the dazzling display below. Or white roses, except that the white garden was already full of them. But he wanted an ultimate experience. Anything low key would be dismissed out of hand.

"I shall need time to think about this," she said.

He gave a short barking laugh. "I don't wonder, it's a real teaser, isn't it? Come in and have some lunch to give you ideas."

The stable yard was crowded with tourists. Standing by the entrance to the house was an outstandingly handsome man, who looked like an outdated sex symbol of the nineteen-fifties, with dark neatly cut hair, very blue eyes, a blazer and well-pressed slacks. He smiled winningly and said, "Good-morning, m'lord."

"Oh, it's you," said Clandon. "On business, are you? What d'you want?"

"The American tour tomorrow wants its lunch booking changed from one to half-past twelve."

"Talk to the catering manageress, she's the proper person," said Clandon roughly and swept past him into the house.

"Who was that?" Celia asked as they mounted the stone stairs.

"His name's Martindale. In the travel business. Makes a bit of a nuisance of himself."

Celia wondered why answering when asked his business made Martindale a nuisance. There must be more to this than met the eye.

Clandon took her straight to the dining room. His wife was already there with their son, a rather plain child of about four with freckles and bright red hair. He ran straight to his father who lifted him high into the air. "Hullo there Simon. And what have you been up to this morning?"

Simon had spent the morning at playschool, and reported that he had drawn a picture of a pig. As Clandon took a profound interest in the pig, Celia saw a different aspect of him, as a gentle and affectionate father who could converse with a child on its own wavelength without lapsing into baby talk.

Presently he looked at his watch. "Where are the others, Harriet?"

"They'll be here in a minute, it's only just one."

After a short delay a tall, slim blonde with a high colour hurried into the room and murmured an apology. As she took her place at the table, Celia decided that her sulky expression of discontent was habitual and permanent. But it was overlaid by some temporary amd immediate cause of annoyance.

"Ah," said Clandon. "My daughter Lady Clara Williamson. Mrs Grant, who is going to be enormously helpful to us over the garden. Aren't you, Mrs Grant?"

Celia, still at a loss to devise an ultimate experience for him, was far from sure.

Clara's air of silent discontent cast a chill over the room. What was her grievance? Celia wondered. As a child of her father's first marriage she might well have resented the arrival of a second wife, little older than herself, and Harriet's production of Simon must have been a severe shock. Till then she (and her sister; why was she not here too?) had no doubt expected to inherit Winthrop jointly. But Simon, as the eldest son of an earl, was already Viscount something or other and the future owner of the estate, while they were merely entitled to daughters' shares. Any woman of spirit would be furious at being ousted by him for no better reason than the fact that he was not a girl.

But Clara was married to someone called Williamson. What had happened, and where was he? Was that what accounted for her depressed state? Or was there some more recent cause? She was a fidgety mass of nerves.

"Ah, there you are," said Clandon in reproof at unpunctuality as George Glenville hurried into the room with an air of fussy efficiency. His face was no longer red with fury, but blotchy and so clean-shaven that it looked as if it hurt. Reactions from the others suggested that he was not welcome, but had a right to his place at the table. Presumably the guides and staff of lower status ate in the cafeteria downstairs, whereas he lunched with the family as an estate manager's perk.

14

"Sorry," he explained, slipping into his place. "I had Webster on the phone about the lease of Glebe Farm, and couldn't get rid of him. He wants us to extend it, Charles, for another—"

"We'll discuss that later in the business room, if you want to," interrupted Clandon icily. Clearly, they were still at daggers drawn.

Glenville subsided and darted nervous little glances round the table from behind his rimless spectacles. Clara seemed particularly irritated by his arrival and pushed food around on her plate with downcast eyes, as if searching it for unhygienic foreign bodies. Clandon was making apologetic faces at his wife. She was watching Clara nervously, as if expecting an embarrassing explosion at any moment. Celia felt vaguely that she ought to say something. But the lunch table was an uncharted sea of other people's emotions, and she had no idea what topic, if any, would be safe.

The Clandons began to manufacture the sort of conversation which is needed when appearances have to be kept up in front of an outsider. Celia was cross-examined on the detailed organisation of Archerscroft Nurseries. When this topic was exhausted, they cast around for further neutral ground and invited everyone to become intensely interested in Simon's morning at playschool, his rabbit and something called Jackie which had to be either a pony or a dog. Clara stayed tetchily silent, but Glenville had plucked up courage and joined in. Presently he and Simon were making faces across the table at each other, with the natural result that Simon got over-excited and started behaving unpleasantly with his food.

"Oh really, George!" snapped Harriet Clandon, glaring at Glenville.

Clara suddenly sprang to life. But instead of exploding into tragedy she struck a bright note of light conversation, and said in an artificial drawing-room voice: "Men are hateful bastards, don't you agree, Mrs Grant?"

It was not clear which of the two men she was aiming this at. But Glenville jumped in his chair as if shot, choked on his mouthful and subsided in silence. Clandon remained impassive. As Celia struggled to frame an inoffensive reply he put a hand on Clara's arm. "Unfortunately, my dear, your experience of men has been far from typical."

Clara shot him a look of hate which placed him among the bastards, then rose from her chair and charged out of the room.

As no one offered any explanation or comment, Celia felt it was up to her now to create a diversion. "Mr Glenville, I was wondering if you're one of the Nosterley Glenvilles?"

"Yes, actually. I'm the baronet's younger brother."

"Really? Eve and I were at school together and she was one of my bridesmaids. How are she and Philip?"

A hangdog look appeared behind the rimless spectacles. "I'm sorry, I have no idea. I haven't been on speaking terms with them for six years."

Abashed, Celia decided that this disaster really wasn't her fault. She had tried, and now it was someone else's turn.

After an awkward pause Clandon charged into the breach, with the one topic she had hoped to avoid. "Well, Mrs Grant? Have you thought of an answer to our problem yet?"

Her mind was a blank about it, but it was socially impossible to say "No" and leave it at that. Something had to be said.

An absurd possibility had just occurred to her, so absurd that she had dismissed it out of hand. But it would do to keep the conversation going. "Well I have had a vague sort of idea."

"Tell us!" he said eagerly.

"There seem to be lots of statues standing about. Have you got a spare one anywhere?"

Clandon thought. "There are some dilapidated bits and pieces down in the frameyard."

"It would have to be male."

"Oh? Do tell us more, Mrs Grant."

"I was thinking that if one put a statue in the grass there, and called it Apollo the sun god, one could have a semicircular bed behind him planted in the colours of the spectrum, to represent a rainbow."

To her horror, he lapped the suggestion up avidly. It was a lunatic idea, and she cursed herself for mentioning it. Carpet bedding in concentric semicircles of red, orange, yellow, green, blue and violet! It would look awful.

"Marvellous!" he cried. "Now why didn't I think of that? But there's only one snag. As far as I know, all the spare statues are female."

After a moment's thought he leapt up from the table and shot out of the room. Glenville excused himself and Harriet Clandon took the opportunity to send Simon off for his afternoon rest. Then she addressed herself to Celia with a mischievous grin. "You looked horrified when Charles took up your rainbow bed idea so avidly. Did you blurt it out without thinking it through? Because you had to say something, anything to fill the gap?"

"That's right. I think it will probably look hideous, like some horror from a municipal park. Shall I try to talk him out of it?"

"No. He's got the bit between his teeth. You wouldn't succeed."

Clandon came back into the room carring an open reference book. "We can use a female statue after all, listen to this: 'Iris, according to mythology was the messenger of the gods, particularly Zeus and Hera. *The rainbow was the path by which she travelled between the gods and men'*."

It would be perfectly simple, he added, to remove one of the semi-draped female statues from the end of Lady Betty's Walk and make it do duty as Iris.

"No really Charles," protested Harriet. "They're much

too matronly. A messenger of the gods needs flying draperies and wings."

"Then we'll have to commission something specially."

Reeling with shock at all this enthusiasm, Celia was further dismayed when she grasped that he wanted this floral abomination planted out at once. "Why not, Mrs Grant? It'll have to be done with bedding plants, why don't we put them in now? Let's go down there and mark out the bed."

"One moment, Charles," Harriet called as he hurried Celia from the room. "Don't forget that you're going to speak to Harding after he's done the three o'clock tour."

"Yes, yes, my dear. Come along, Mrs Grant."

He plunged down the stairs to the basement and out into the yard. It was crowded with sightseers, some of whom recognised him and whispered to each other. Reflecting on the unpleasantness of living in a goldfish bowl surrounded by tourists, Celia struggled to keep up. She saw no real reason why she and Archerscroft should be involved in this disastrous exercise in carpet bedding, and suggested that the gardeners at Winthrop could handle it themselves.

"No no, my dear Mrs Grant. I've only got two full-time men working here, plus a few girls who come in and weed on days when we're not open."

"Surely they can manage?"

"No, really. Bedding out is fiddly, very labour intensive. Besides, I need your expertise. Where am I to get bedding plants from so late in the season?"

Where indeed? If any could be found, he would have to pay through the nose for them.

"You had the idea, you deserve to profit from it," he said firmly. "Why don't I give you a permanent contract to keep the thing in colour through the seasons?"

The prospect filled Celia with horror. "Let's see how well it works out first."

Resigning herself to the inevitable, she collected a notebook and a long tape measure from her car. In

18

a working area screened off by trees from the house Clandon collected a mallet and pegs from a tool shed. They set out down the garden, but on a second view of the site, problems emerged. The planting would be impossibly difficult if tall red plants had to be found for the outer ring, and shorter and shorter ones descending through the colours of the spectrum towards the front. It would be simpler to use bedding plants roughly the same height, but in that case the bed would have to slope forwards to display the ones at the back. How steep would the slope have to be? Would a retaining wall be needed in front, to stop earth being washed forward on to the grass? Should the retaining wall raise the bed so high that it could be seen from the grass path below?

Deciding all this took time, and they were still hard at work with the tape measure when Harriet Clandon appeared on the terrace above. "It's half-past three. I've told Harding you want to see him and he's waiting."

Grunting with displeasure, he hurried off towards the house. His wife hesitated for a moment, then came down the steps to stand beside Celia.

"Don't worry, my dear. It might look rather nice."

"Or utterly vulgar."

"Different, anyway."

"You're right, though. It's no use trying to stop it."

"No. He sweeps one off one's feet, doesn't he? Dead keen to get on with things. It frightens me sometimes. Come in and have some tea."

"Thank you, but I must finish taking my measurements here and then I ought to get back to the office. Would you make my excuses to Lord Clandon? I'll phone him tonight and we'll decide what happens next."

"Oh, do. I'm sure he'll want you back here tomorrow at crack of dawn to carry on the good work."

Having measured up the site, Celia went back to the stable yard, which was filled with a newly arrived busload of old age pensioners. She threaded her way through them and went to her car. As she unlocked it, Harding appeared from one of the stables and ran towards her, shouting, "You bitch, you spy, how dare you tell them lies about me."

He was twice her size and in a very ugly mood. Watched by the pensioners, she climbed into the car quickly, intending to avoid trouble by driving away. But in her agitation she had dropped her keys on the car floor and it took her some minutes to find them, start up and drive off.

She had only gone a few yards before she had to brake to a shuddering halt. Harding was standing a few inches from her front bumper to prevent her escape. She reversed to drive round him, but the alarmed pensioners were everywhere, it would be too dangerous.

Harding came round to the driver's door and wrenched at the handle. She had managed to lock it, so he battered on the window, shouting abuse at her for 'telling lies' that had cost him his job. when she ignored him, he began rocking the car.

The rocking grew more violent. Some of the horrified pensioners began to scream. But they were elderly and afraid to interfere. She started sounding long blasts on her horn to summon help. But she was being thrown from side to side and lost contact with the horn button. By the time she regained it she knew with a chill of fear that he was trying to turn the car over, and would soon succeed.

As it teetered on the point of balance, the rocking slackened, then stopped. Peering out, she saw that George Glenville had come to the rescue. Though he was much shorter and lighter than Harding, he was dealing with him very efficiently, tackling him from behind and pinioning his arms to his side. Locked together, they staggered around the yard till Glenville managed to bang Harding's forehead hard against the stonework of the stables.

He slumped to the floor, bleeding heavily, but instead of leaving him alone Glenville continued the attack, banging his head again and again on the cobbles of the yard. Then, standing over him, he kicked him viciously in the stomach several times.

As Celia climbed shakily out of her car, he brushed his hands together efficiently to mark the end of a job well done, and stood basking in the admiration of the pensioners while he waited for her to thank him. Sickened as much by the brutality of her rescue as by the shock of Harding's brutal attack, she managed to say how grateful she was.

Glenville grinned. "I was in my office over the stables, lucky I heard you."

"Oh. Thank you again."

"It was a pleasure."

He was absolutely right, she decided in disgust. It had been a pleasure. He was a brute and had enjoyed every minute of it.

Chapter Two

Harding was still writhing in agony on the ground. "Will he be all right?" Celia asked.

Glenville's grin broadened unpleasantly. "There's no damage that a bit of sticking plaster won't cure."

"Well, have you got any sticking plaster?" she asked.

"Yes. But you're bleeding. Let me attend to you first."

Blood was indeed trickling down from a cut above her ear, inflicted while the car was being rocked.

"The first aid box is in the office," he said. "Come on up and I'll deal with it."

"No!" She was filled with revulsion. Even if bleeding to death, she would not let him touch her. "I'll get help in the house."

Before he could protest, she made a dash for the service entrance. Before she reached it, Harriet Clandon called from a window above. "Come on up, Mrs Grant, I'll deal with it."

Meeting Celia at the entrance to the private wing, she said: "Goodness, what a to-do, are you all right apart from that cut?"

"I think so," Celia replied shakily.

"I kept telling Charles that Peter Harding was stark staring mad, but he wouldn't listen. I'm glad George rescued you, but as usual he overdid being efficient."

Her first aid kit was in her bathroom. Within minutes she had bathed and cleaned the cut and examined it. "I don't think it'll need stitches, in fact the bleeding's stopping already. Let's give it a few minutes, then I'll dress it and put on sticking plaster."

"Thank you. I suppose I should have let Mr Glenville attend to it."

"Brrr. I'd rather die than let George touch me," said Harriet. "How interesting that you felt the same thing."

"It was instinctive, Lady Clandon. I don't know why."

"Oh, do call me Harriet, all my friends do, and you're—?"

"Celia."

Harriet broke into a mischievous grin. "Wasn't lunch awful? Disaster after disaster. Half-way through I even wondered whether it would help if I spilt something over myself."

"Quite a lot seemed to be going on."

"I know, but what? Had Clara and Charles had a row?"

"He and Mr Glenville certainly had," said Celia. "It was still rumbling on in the business room when I arrived."

"What about, I wonder? I must try to find out."

"Something to do with running the estate, perhaps?"

"Probably. Charles can be very obstinate when he's made up his mind. Last year he insisted on rebuilding the Gothic ruin at vast expense and nothing I could say would stop him. Oh dear, it worries me, the way we're spending all this money."

Celia maintained a sympathetic silence.

"I hadn't expected anything like this," Harriet went on. "When we got married the nuns were here. We lived in a cosy little farmhouse on the estate. Charles got on with his work for charities and I kept house. Then Simon was born, and everything changed. Charles decided to move back here and restore the place to its former glory so that he could hand it on in good shape to the future Fifteenth Earl."

"Does Simon know yet what's in store for him?"

"No."

23

"What happens later, if he decides he doesn't want to be saddled with it?"

"I shudder to think," said Harriet. "Charles dotes on him. He'd be furious if Simon didn't come up to scratch."

"But he's only four. You needn't cross that bridge till you come to it."

"My trouble is, I always see bridges a long way ahead."

"That's wise, but one mustn't let the prospect of crossing them make one miserable."

She gave Celia's arm a grateful squeeze. "Oh, what a relief it is to have someone like you to talk to. I'm devoted to Charles, but he's so much older and I'm a bit awestruck."

And there was no one else to confide in, Celia realised. Glenville was in some mysterious doghouse, and Clara carried around a ticking bomb of her own misery.

"Your stepdaughter seems very unhappy," she remarked.

"Yes, it's a very sad story. James Williamson was a director of a huge supranational conglomerate, and for two years they'd been living in Texas, just outside Houston. He'd collected their little girl from playschool, and on the way home they were both killed in a frightful car smash."

"Horrors. When was this?"

"Three months ago, and as they'd sold their house in England, she'd nowhere to go. So of course we said she should come here till she'd decided what to do. But she's completely shut in on herself. I've been trying to get through to her, but it's no good."

"Does she resent you for being her stepmother?"

"No, I don't think it's that. She was married before I came on the scene, and James left her very well off. So even the shock of Simon's arrival wasn't as great as it might have been."

"But there's another daughter by your husband's first marriage, isn't there?"

"Oh dear yes, Susan's a different story. She's living in a flat in Beckley with a very undesirable young man, and it seems to be my fault that she ran away from home. She hates all this prettification of Winthrop, and thinks I forced Charles into doing it. I'm the scheming dowager who's feathering the nest for her spoilt brat."

"How awful. I hope she's not on drugs."

"I wouldn't know, I never see her. Celia, do please be patient with Charles and keep the lines open so that you can go on coming here. I really do need a friend."

"I'll do my best."

"Oh, thank you. That cut's stopped bleeding now. I'll dress it. D'you feel fit to drive home, or would you like to stay the night?"

"Thank you, but I'm quite okay now."

"Good, then we'll see you tomorrow."

Next morning Celia braced herself to confess to Bill Wilkins, her partner and head gardener, that a rash remark over lunch had landed Archerscroft with a commission which filled her with disgust. She found him looking frustrated. One of the new girls, overwhelmed by his blond good looks, had been making adoring eyes at him. This sort of thing happened at regular intervals. But the dramatic death of his steady girlfriend had left him puritanical about sex. His usual technique for ridding himself of these lovelorn maidens was to behave so brutally to them that they resigned in floods of tears. But it was the height of the early summer season. Archerscroft was short-handed, and Celia had laid down the law. He must behave himself and treat the girl gently. She could not be spared.

When told that they were confronted with the task of planting out a rainbow he was by no means as appalled as she expected.

"Oh Celia, don't be so snobby. Carpet bedding's coming back in, we got to move with the times."

"But not at breakneck speed. He wants it done now, this instant. I phoned him last night and tried to talk him into waiting till the autumn, but it was no good."

Bill pulled a long face. "We'll have to buy in full-grown plants."

"Yes. Goodness knows what they'll cost."

"That's okay Celia, provided he pays."

"I wish I could be sure he will. And think what nasty plants! Hundreds of hideous scarlet pelargoniums for the back row, then millions of horrid French marigolds in orange and yellow, and horrors, what is there that's green that won't wreck the effect by having flowers?"

"Grass."

"Too short if you mow it and too straggly if you don't."

"*Hosta lancifolia* then. It don't flower till the autumn, and even then they're so small, they won't show."

"And what will it all look like when we've finished?"

"Quite nice, I reckon. The coach parties will love it."

Celia spent an unhappy morning ringing around the trade to find out what bedding plants were available, then made scale drawings of the rainbow bed and set off to Winthrop to get them approved by Clandon. He insisted on taking her down to check her measurements on the site, which he had roped off because it was another of the days when the garden was open to the public. As they wielded their tape measure and hammered in pegs a small crowd of gapers gathered to watch.

To be effective the bed would have to be built on a slope, and the next question was how high it should be raised. They stuck in stakes of varying height, and retreated down the central vista to study the effect. Even from the lawn by the river at the bottom, it could not be seen.

Clandon hesitated. "How about raising it a bit more, so that they see it from down here?"

In Celia's opinion this gaudy horror should be kept hidden from the public till the last possible moment. "Wouldn't it be better to let it burst upon the view as a glorious surprise when people get to the top of the steps?"

"Perhaps you're right, Mrs Grant."

But would the glorious surprise not be visible from other parts of the garden? Trying out the possible viewpoints, they had to pass the cornus beds, neatly laid out with a cast-iron name plate stuck in the ground beside each specimen. Celia paused to admire a thriving one which was in flower, with enormous bracts maturing from green to white, then fading to pink. But if the name plate was right, the flowers were too big, the leaves too pale a green, and their margins had no business to undulate. It was not *Cornus kousa canadensis* as the name plate alleged, but *C. kousa chinensis* whose name plate adorned a less spectacular specimen of *C. canadensis* a few yards away.

Would it be tactless to point this out? Before she could decide, Clandon had made a similar discovery himself. To judge from the labelling *C. controversa variegata* had plain green leaves, whereas those of *C. controversa* itself were hectically variegated in white and yellow.

Further investigation showed that the labels had been switched on all the cultivars of *C. florida*, and indeed on almost all the cornuses in the collection. Uttering little exclamations of concern Clandon began putting things right.

"Who on earth would play a trick like that?" asked Celia as she helped him. He looked at her gloomily and shrugged, but did not answer.

As they walked back up the garden, Harriet Clandon came hurrying down the central vista to meet them.

"Security alert," she told him. "A couple that George suspects of spying for one of the gangs."

He reacted sharply. "Where? Just now? Have they gone?"

"I don't know. George rushed off to the car park in case their car's still there."

"What alerted you?"

"They were in the stable yard. George spotted them and fetched me. The man had some field glasses, to see where to cut the wires for the telephone and burglar alarm and floodlights. A few minutes earlier he'd caught the same two in the private wing, pretending to be looking for a lavatory."

"Hoping to get a glimpse of the alarm system's control panel," Clandon commented. "What did they look like?"

"Elderly. Rather a lot of clothes for the time of year. He had a bad leg and a walking-stick with a rubber tip."

"Which tour were they on?"

"Probably the four o'clock. Or it could have been the three-thirty if they went to the tea-shop afterwards."

"Get both the guides to come to see me when they've finished their tours. And go round the house yourself and see if anything's missing."

She hurried off and Clandon turned gloomily to Celia. "This is one of the things we have to live with. These people are quite determined and very clever. They send someone round to see where the real valuables are and find out about the security system. A week or two later they strike, and things that have been in your family for generations are on sale within twenty-four hours in Amsterdam."

"And you think these people were on a reconnaissance?"

"Yes, if they were looking at the wiring. You can find out quite a lot if you keep your eyes open on the way round."

"But . . . an elderly couple? A man with a gammy leg?"

"That does surprise me a little. It's usually part of a different game. They hang back because he can't walk fast, and when the guide has gone into the next room, they pinch something. We know better now, the guide always goes out last. But we lost a gilt presentation sword that way, a gift to the Tenth Earl from a regiment he'd raised. It vanished down an allegedly lame man's trouser leg."

"But would they send a lame man if it was a reconnaissance?"

Clandon hesitated. "Probably not. I rather hope something small's missing. That will mean we needn't expect the attentions of one of the big gangs."

They were back in the stable yard. Deciding that he would not want her there in such a moment of crisis she headed for her car, but he called her back.

"Do stay. We haven't settled the details of your contract. Let me deal with this tiresome business first, then we'll talk."

But he was clearly preoccupied, and Celia doubted if anything worthwhile could be settled that night. It was difficult to say so and go home, so she followed him in. He led her up the stairs from the basement, along the corridor above, and out through the door at the end of it into the entrance hall. The last tour of the day had already started. The room was empty except for a man counting money at the ticket desk. Questioned by Clandon, he replied that he vaguely remembered a lame man accompanied by a woman, and was pretty sure they had joined the four o'clock tour. But a lot of people had come in to join it, and he had been too busy selling tickets to take much notice.

"Who took that tour?" Clandon asked.

"Mrs Patterson, my lord. She knows you want to see her."

"The important thing now," Clandon muttered to Celia, "is to get an accurate description." He hurried back into

29

the private wing and paused outside the sitting room. "Wait in there. I'll go downstairs and see if anyone in the shop or tea-room remembers them."

In the sitting room she found a tray of tea, and also Clara, who was drowning her sorrows in a Catherine Cookson novel. She looked up from it when she saw Celia and said in a graveyard tone: "Hullo. Aren't they coming in for their tea?"

"They're busy for the moment. There's a security scare on."

"Oh. Then we'd better have some before it gets stewed." She poured tea for herself and Celia, looked at her but could think of nothing to say, and went back to her novel.

Some time passed before Clandon returned. No one in the shop or tea-room remembered the suspect pair. A gardener working on the garden side of the house had seen an elderly couple, a lame man and and a woman standing on the terrace. He could provide no detailed description, but was sure that they had gone back to the car park without exploring the garden.

There was a knock at the door and a pleasant looking grey-haired woman came in.

"Ah, Mrs Patterson," said Clandon "Do sit down. You took the four o'clock tour?"

"That's right, and I've talked to Lady Clandon. I remember the couple she means quite well. After that business with the sword, we always pay special attention to anyone who seems to be lame."

"Good. Now can you please describe them to me, as accurately as possible?"

"Let me see now. He was rather bald, with a fringe of longish, not very clean grey hair round the sides and back. Not very healthy looking, his skin was rather yellow, and – yes, he had one of those dark blotches that elderly people sometimes have, on his cheek."

"Well done, Mrs Patterson. Which cheek?"

"I'm sorry, I don't remember."

Noting all this down, Clandon questioned her about the man's height and build and the details of his clothes, then made her describe the woman with him. "Rather dumpy with a fattish face and thick glasses. Grey hair, I don't think it was a wig. Judging from the way she peered at things, she must have been very short-sighted. And she had on a sort of loose baggy sweater. You'd think she'd be too hot."

"Did they behave at all suspiciously?"

"Not as far as I could see. But it was a very large group, over thirty, and I couldn't keep my eye on them all the time."

Harriet hurried into the room. "Damn all men with bad legs," she began, then saw Mrs Patterson and spoke more gently. "I'm afraid one of the little Sevres vases is missing, from the console table in the music room."

Mrs Patterson rose with a cry of distress. "Oh how awful, I'm so sorry!"

"Don't worry, Mrs Patterson," said Clandon quickly. "These things happen, it's not your fault."

"It was such a large group," she stammered, and began to cry.

"Please don't distress yourself," he went on. "I'm rather glad they turned out to be pilferers. We were afraid they might be the advance guard of one of the big gangs. Harriet, give Mrs Patterson some tea."

George Glenville bustled in, very much in control of the situation. "No luck, I'm afraid, they'd gone, but only just. Several people in the car park remembered seeing them. Their car was a Ford Fiesta, rather battered, with a G registration. The people who'd been parked next to them were still there having a picnic tea, and gave me quite a good description."

Clandon noted down the details, which confirmed those given by Mrs Patterson but omitted the dark blotch on the man's cheek.

31

"You didn't notice it?" Clandon asked him. "You saw them, and so did Harriet."

"Only from the window of the business room," Harriet explained. "Not close to."

Clandon consulted the notes he had made. "Not a bad description. If neither of you can add anything I'll phone Ripley straight away."

"I'll go," volunteered Glenville.

Ignoring this, Clandon headed for the door.

"Why don't you let me?" Glenville protested. "You've enough on your plate."

If he hoped to ingratiate himself after the previous day's quarrel, he was doomed to disappointment. Clandon looked at him coldly and disappeared into the business room to telephone. As Harriet was still devoting herself to Mrs Patterson, and Clara had taken refuge in her book, Glenville felt obliged to entertain Celia.

"Looking after a place like this is a desperate business nowadays," he began. "These people are very well organised: everything they do is planned like a military operation. They have ways of dealing with the most sophisticated security alarms, and the pundits say one ought to put one's Fabergé eggs or whatever in the safe every night if one doesn't want to lose them. But what can you do with a corridor lined with Chelsea and Bow figurines worth several millions? The show cases are all alarmed separately of course, but that wouldn't really stop them."

"What about that extraordinary gilt object on the dining room table?"

"Oh, the Augsburg *surtout de table*. You're right, it's the most valuable single object we've got. Charles puts it in the safe every night, but everything else has to take pot luck."

"What sort of people are they?" Celia asked.

"Pretty ruthless big-business types with international money-laundering connections. At least one lot are teamed up with a major drug ring in Amsterdam, and until Northern Ireland quieted down the Protestant paramilitaries there were involved: it was one of the ways they financed their arms purchases. Nowadays the police art squads take thefts from houses like this very seriously, but there's a limit to what they can do. They give you advice on security, and they investigate very thoroughly after the event. But until disaster strikes you're really on your own."

"Are there alarms in the grounds?"

"No, only security lights; you can't surround the place with barbed wire. The best defence we have is intelligence, and that's very well organised, thanks to the chap at Ripley Castle in Yorkshire, a man called Ingilby. He set up an informal arrangement with other nearby houses open to the public. They would phone each other when they lost anything to pilferers or had visits from suspicious characters, in case the same people turned up elsewhere. The police thought it was a grand idea, an intelligence network that wasn't costing them anything, so they encouraged Ingilby to expand it and now it's more or less nationwide."

"So your two can be arrested if they turn up at another house?" Celia suggested.

"Only if they're caught pinching something, that's the snag. We've no evidence that they took that vase."

"I feel awful about it, Lady Clandon," moaned Mrs Patterson.

"Don't worry, my dear, a vase is only a vase, it might have been much worse. If they stole something, it means they were only pilferers, not the advance guard of the stocking-mask brigade."

Glenville frowned. "Yes, but I wish we hadn't seen them reconnoitring the security alarm."

Celia had been right in thinking that there would be no serious discussion that night of the contractual arrangements for her work in the garden. When she tried to tie the situation up next morning on the telephone, Clandon turned out to have had maddening second thoughts. Would it not be better after all to let the rainbow shed its radiance over the whole garden? The statue of Iris would be visible from a distance anyway. Could she please come over and look at the sight lines again?

She agreed reluctantly. By mid-morning she and Clandon were sticking yet more stakes into the site of the bed, and viewing the result from all angles. It soon became clear that he was determined to have the bed raised so that it could be seen far and wide. She pointed out that this would involve barrowing in massive quantities of extra topsoil, and building a retaining wall at the front of the bed. But he was unshaken.

Determined to get the business side of the operation tied up, she sat him down on a bench, altered her estimate to cover the cost of the wall and the extra topsoil, and presented it to him. He agreed it at once, stipulating only that the work should be started as soon as possible after the weekend.

They were down by the river and their route back to the house took them past the cornus beds. Celia gave it a glance, then halted. *Cornus kousa chinensis* had become Canadian again, and vice versa. Yesterday's interference had been repeated. Over half the name plates had been switched.

"Is this someone's idea of a joke?" she asked Clandon.

He gave her one of his uncomfortable looks. "Yes, but I think I know who's behind it. Let's just put it right quietly, shall we? I don't want a great fuss."

They did so, watched by a group of inscrutable Japanese tourists.

Back at the house Celia was unlocking her car when Harriet Clandon came out into the yard to invite her to stay to lunch. Being genuinely too busy, she declined, and was about to drive off when a large coach party came into the yard. These, to judge from their speech and their slightly odd holiday clothing, were Martindale's Americans on their way to lunch in the restaurant. He was acting as their courier, and as he passed the Clandons he greeted them politely. Harriet turned her back on him at once. Clandon glared. A faint smile appeared on Martindale's over-handsome face, as if this display of hostility amused him.

Celia spent the weekend catching up on neglected business. Early on Monday morning she set off for Winthrop, followed by Bill driving a tip-up truck full of York stone with which to build the retaining wall. Owing to the narrowness of the paths in the garden, it could not be driven to the site of the bed, so he dumped the stone in the screened-off working area where tools and garden machinery were kept. It would have to be moved to the site bit by bit in a trailer behind a garden tractor.

Clandon's two gardeners had been detailed to help Bill prepare the site. One of them, Kevin Watts, was in his twenties, fair-haired, with a reddish congested face and a heavy body which would one day be a shapeless cascade of middle-aged fat. The other gardener, Harry Garton, was older, wiry and hungry-looking, with dark hair grizzled at the temples.

Celia produced her drawings and explained what had to be done. Bill was good with staff (other than lovesick maidens) and she was soon able to leave the three men working harmoniously together. But before starting back to Archerscroft she decided to see if the cornus beds had been interfered with over the weekend.

All seemed to be in order there. But down by the river, something was moving. She went down to the water's edge and looked along the bank. Over to her right, a rubber dinghy was moored in the reeds. Two people, a young man and a girl, were landing from it and heading past the cornus beds into the woodland beyond.

Celia followed. The couple heard her footsteps behind

them on the dry twigs and turned. The young man was well-built, scruffily dressed and unshaven, unless what was on view could be classed as designer stubble. The girl was mousy-haired with strangely pale eyes. She too was in scruffy jeans and they both wore dirty T-shirts with environmental slogans printed across the chests.

"May I ask what you doing here?" asked the girl in surprising upper-class tones. "The garden doesn't open to the public till eleven."

"I'm not a member of the public," said Celia.

"Really? Who are you then?"

"I might ask you the same question."

"I am Lady Susan Winthrop, this is my father's garden and Ron here is my live-in lover. And now, if I may ask, who the hell are you?"

"Your father's employing me to work in the garden."

"Ah yes, in this Borgia garden, this filthy tourist trap that pollutes the river with poisonous chemicals."

"I'm sure he uses chemicals as carefully as every responsible gardener does nowadays."

"Why use them at all? Black spot doesn't do any harm to roses."

"I dare say. But the public doesn't like to see it."

Lady Susan's vehemence drove her accent sharply down market. "Who cares about the bloody public? It sickens me, what's happening here. It's my vampire of a stepmother's fault. She's made my dad spend millions to prop up this useless great barracks of a house, so that it can be handed on as a dodgy commercial concern to her brat. Poor little Simon will have to look after it when Dad dies, whether he likes it or not."

Celia sympathised with this point of view, but saw no point in saying so.

"How dare you help him fix up this obscene horticultural fun fair?" she continued furiously. "It's disgusting, it's as dead and artificial as plastic flowers on graves, and doesn't even produce anything to eat."

"Then why do you come here?"

"To exorcise its demons. There's a little building over there in the wood called the Temple of Flora. Ron and I go in there from time to time to propitiate the poor little goddess by having a good hearty fuck."

"Thass what Sue and I do in there," said Ron, with his hands suggestively low on his hips. "You can come and watch if you like."

"Thank you, but I discovered about the bees and the birds and the rabbits some time ago."

"Then if I may make a suggestion," shouted Susan, "why don't you bugger off?"

As Celia retreated she passed the cornus beds. All was in order there for the moment, but it was clear now who had interfered with them, and why Susan's father did not want a fuss made about it.

At the work site they were digging a trench for the foundations of the retaining wall. Harry Garton had seen the rubber dinghy arrive. As he lowered his grizzled head to load one of the turves they had lifted into a wheelbarrow he muttered to Kevin: "Susie's back at the temple. She and her feller will be at it again."

"Is that what they do in there?" said Kevin.

"Sure. Her feller's got a damn great ding-dong on him, like a donkey's."

Kevin's round red face broke into a grin. "You been watching them, you filthy bugger."

"I like knowing what goes on."

"Such as?" Kevin queried.

"Jack Martindale's at it as usual. There's the new barmaid at the Winthrop Arms, and the nice little Italian waitress at that restaurant on the Beckley Road."

"Go on with you, Harry, you made all this up."

"No, it's true. You'd think all that shaggin' would kill him, but he seems okay. The other day he even had a go at Lady Clara up at the house, but she wasn't having any, so—"

"Careful, that's enough of that," Bill muttered crossly as Lord Clandon hove into sight. He had intercepted Celia on her way out and brought her with him on a visit of inspection. The two Winthrop gardeners treated him with a feudal respect which Bill found astonishing. After he had made various futile suggestions for changing the design, which Celia dealt with firmly, she removed him and took herself off to Archerscroft, leaving Bill in charge.

"She's okay, your boss is," said Kevin when they had gone. "Told him off good and proper."

"He's mad," added Harry. "Starts you on a job, then takes you off it to do something else. Half-way through that he says no, he wants it done different, and you have to start all over again."

"I hate the bastard," muttered Kevin.

Though their language was sometimes foul, he and Harry were hard workers. By lunch time the trench for the foundations of the wall had been dug and a trailer with the first load of York stone had been brought in. For lunch they drove to a pub in the village in Kevin's dilapidated car.

"You don't eat up at the house?" Bill asked them.

"No fear," said Kevin. "Too many spies there: you can't say a thing. They'll report you to his nibs soon as look at you. Terrified of him, that's what they are."

"He's a holy terror," Harry agreed. "Talk about strait-laced! Cor! No nasty language, and sex is something you do with your wife if you've got one, otherwise you keep the whole bag of tricks to yourself. Put a foot wrong there, and he's down on you like a ton of bricks."

"I hate the bastard," growled Kevin. "Her Ladyship's okay though. Quite good to look at too."

"Not that dishy," Harry objected.

"Oh, she's not bad. I wouldn't mind."

Garton took a pull at his beer. "Jack Martindale didn't mind either." He turned to Bill. "You know that story?"

Bill had been listening with puritanical disapproval. But in the interests of good working relations, he decided not to choke him off.

Harry launched into his recital with relish. "Six – seven year ago it was. Her Ladyship wasn't Her Ladyship then, she was plain Miss Evans what taught in the village school and went to church every Sunday because His Lordship that was chairman of the governors of the school said she better had or else."

"I hate the bastard," intoned Kevin like a monotonous Greek chorus.

"And then this handsome Mr Martindale comes along. Little Miss Evans don't know he's the champion red hot poker of Hampshire, so when he unzips his flies she decides he's the love of her life. And one day Jack's ugly old wife, who's a magistrate, goes off to some conference and this is their chance. But the conference was all about how you must be kind to criminals and not flog them, which is what she likes to do. So she's fed up and comes away before the end. Of course she's not expected home, and when she goes upstairs, there are the two of them, going at it hammer and tongs in her bed."

After a pause for Rabelaisian laughter Harry went on. "So next day Mrs Martindale, she goes to the school and bursts into the classroom where Miss Evans is teaching and she shouts, "You filthy whore!" and suchlike, and it's the top class, ten and eleven year olds, and they all love it, especially when Mrs Martindale brings out a nightdress that's all crumpled and brandishes it under Miss Evans' nose and says 'How dare you leave this in my bed, you little tart?' And Miss Evans bursts into tears and runs out of the classroom and never goes near the school again."

"Go on," mocked Kevin. "You made all this up."

"You ask anyone. The whole village knew."

"I didn't," Kevin objected.

"You was just a kid."

"There is something, though," said Kevin thoughtfully.

"When Martindale goes up to the big house for his travel business, she behaves as if he was a bad smell."

"You see? And His Lordship does too. She's all prim and proper now, but when you look at it, she's no better than she should be."

Bill, who had been listening to all this with half an ear, decided that it was nonsense. A strait-laced aristocrat like Clandon would never dream of marrying a tainted bit of goods from his own village. The whole story must have been conjured out of the air by Harry's dirty mind.

"Cor, look at the time," said Harry, alarmed. "He's strict on timekeeping, we better get back."

"I hate the bastard," moaned Kevin.

On the way out to the car, he held Bill back. "You know what, Kevin's in bad with the boss because he's landed a girl with a bundle. He says Kevin's got to marry her and if he doesn't he'll fire him."

"You can't fire a man for that. Kevin could take him to court."

Harry gave him a sidelong look. "His Bloody Lordship would find a way. He's clever and he's mean."

When they knocked off work at four, the foundations of the retaining wall had been laid. All the York stone was piled up on the site, ready to build the retaining wall, and they had started bringing in topsoil.

In the morning they were hard at it soon after by half-past eight. At nine Lady Clandon appeared on the terrace above, and looked down at them.

"Morning, my lady," said Harry and Kevin in unison.

"I thought my husband might be here. You haven't seen him?"

"No, my lady."

"He didn't come in for breakfast. I wonder where he's got to."

By ten o'clock the alarm in the household was general. "He can't have gone far," said George Glenville. "His car's still here."

"He got up early, and said he was going down the garden," Harriet told him. "He's done that several times in the past few days, before the gardeners arrive."

Glenville looked worried. "Better organise a search, hadn't we?"

"I suppose so. But quietly, without a huge fuss. He'll be furious if we have the whole staff beating the undergrowth, and he's just fallen asleep under a tree."

Organised with bustling efficiency by Glenville, the gardeners searched the garden and the woodland beyond. But Lord Clandon was nowhere in the grounds.

One of Kevin Watts' hobbies was coarse fishing. When he began searching the woodland down by the river, he paid close attention to the water below the river bank, and very little to the cornus beds on the other side of the path. That was why he found The Fourteenth Earl of Clandon, lying face down in the reeds near the bank with his head bashed in.

Chapter Three

Everything seemed normal at Winthrop when Celia arrived at mid-morning to check progress at the site, except that a police car was parked in front of the main entrance. But there were two more police cars in the stable yard, and a constable was guarding the basement door.

She approached him. "Oh dear, what's happened?"

"A death, madam, I'm sorry to say."

"Horrors. Who?"

"The Earl of Clandon."

She stared at him, numb with shock. Shamingly, her first thought was for herself, not Harriet. There would be no need for this hefty police presence if Clandon had died peacefully in his bed. Why do these things wait to happen till I'm around, she asked herself. It's ghoulish. I'm a bird of ill omen, like one of those television war reporters that one views with horror when they appear in yet another corpse-strewn world trouble spot.

But this time she would stay out of it, look the other way. If anyone hinted that she had occasionally helped the police with their enquires she would deny it.

Only after reaching this decision did she remember to feel desperately sorry for Harriet Clandon.

"If you're employed in the house," said the policeman, "I'd better let you in."

"No. No thank you, I only deal with the garden. I must contact some people who work there."

"I'm sorry, no one is allowed into the garden at present."

"Then where are the gardeners?"

"Inside, madam, with the other employees that the inspector will want to question. I think you'll find them in the tea-room."

Bill was sitting in the cafeteria, at a table with the two staff gardeners, Garton and Watts.

"Bill, d'you know what's happened to Lord Clandon?" she asked.

"He was in the river. Kevin here found him."

"That's right," said Watts, looking queasy but self-important, "with his head bashed in. The water was all bloody."

Bill rose to confront her. "So here you go again, rooting for clues."

"No I don't. Murder horrifies me, and I don't owe these people anything. I want nothing to do with it."

"Oh Celia, you always say that, and ten minutes later you're like a dog sniffing around after the heroin."

Suddenly she was furious with him. "That's not funny. Listen, Bill. The police here don't know me, and Harriet Clandon thinks I'm just a lady gardener who makes unwise remarks about carpet bedding. Nobody will ask me for an opinion, and I certainly shan't volunteer one."

He looked at her doubtfully. "You watch out, Celia. I know you."

"No you don't. I'm going straight back to Archerscroft, and you can join me there when the police say you can."

But before she reached the door Mrs Holland, the Clandons' housekeeper, intercepted her. "Oh Mrs Grant, her Ladyship's been asking for you, and I saw your car in the yard. She says, would you go to her as soon as you can?"

"Oh. Yes, of course."

Bill made her a mocking I-told-you-so grimace.

"Don't make faces at me like that," she said crossly. "I'm only being sent for to dispense sympathy and comfort."

Upstairs, Harriet sat huddled in a corner of the sofa, staring into space. "Hullo, Celia," she said dully. "Bless you for coming. I knew you would."

"My poor Harriet, what can I say? Except that I'm desperately sorry." She sat down beside her and they held hands. Neither spoke. For the moment this seemed to be comfort enough.

A sudden thought struck Celia. "Where's Simon?"

"At playschool in the village. I've asked them not to tell him till he gets home."

They lapsed back into silence. It lasted till the door opened and Clara came in. "There's a woman on the phone from the social services. She says she wants to come and counsel you."

"How dare she?" cried Harriet, sitting bolt upright. "What impertinence, tell her to go and counsel whoever had this absurd idea."

Clara surveyed her from the doorway. "Now you know what it feels like to be a widow. Not sad. Just angry."

When she had gone Harriet said: "Actually she's wrong. I don't feel anything yet, I wish I did." After a long silence she added: "Oh dear, I didn't realise Clara hated me so much."

"Does she? She strikes me as too full of her own problems to grasp that other people actually exist."

"What are her problems, though?" Harriet frowned. "I've never understood what makes her tick, and Charles never discussed her with me. He kept her and Susan in a separate compartment because they're only my stepchildren. That was one of the things that made life difficult."

"She obviously misses her husband a lot."

"Goodness no, she'd have buried him in a plague pit if she could have found one. Don't tell anyone because it's a family secret, but it was awful, what he did. Jessica, their little girl, had just started school, she was five. Clara was at the hairdresser, so James

44

went to collect her and drive her home, but he was drunk. That was why he smashed up the car and killed them both."

"Horrors," said Celia. "Is that why she says she hates men?"

Harriet gave her a strange look which she could not interpret. "Clara doted on Jessica. She'll never forgive James."

The door opened and Mrs Holland came in, wearing an expression of horrified distaste. "Mr Martindale is here, my lady."

"Mr Martindale? I don't believe it. Tell him to go away at once."

"He wants to know if we're opening to the public as usual today."

"How should I know? Tell him to go and ask the police."

When Mrs Holland had gone she made a disgusted face.

"You don't like him," Celia concluded.

"No. Jack Martindale is Hampshire's self-appointed Fornicator-in-Chief. No village maiden is safe from him. His wife divorced him for that, and he's been rocketing round the district ever since like a loose cannon, looking for another rich woman to marry. There are no takers so far, though."

"You'd think some idiotic female would marry him for his looks."

"And have the church full of betrayed shopgirls in floods of tears? No. Clara's disaster of a husband left her with five million, so Jack tried to get a nibble out of her. But she bit his head off in one mouthful."

The door flew open and George Glenville burst into the room. "Harriet, I'm sorry to bother you, but the police say Charles's keys weren't on him. They're probably in his dressing-room, can I have them?"

"Why? You've got your own key to the safe."

"There may be things in his desk that need attending to."

"If there are, the solicitors can deal with them when they come."

"Suppose there's something urgent?"

Harriet stared at him coldly. "Please go and be efficient somewhere else."

When he had gone she threw Celia a rueful look. "Oh dear. Bereavement seems to have made me very bad-tempered."

"I see why he gets on your nerves."

She nodded. "He reminds me of a ferret. Or a weasel. Some fierce little hunting animal anyway. Celia, can I ask you to do me a big favour? Would you mind awfully sleeping here tonight?"

"I'll have to go back to the office first, I've things to attend to. But of course I will, if it would help."

"Oh, thank you, it would. Charles was my only defence against feeling lonely, and now I've got nobody. Simon's too little. Come as soon as you can, I need moral support amid all this police fuss."

A fuss of some kind was going on outside in the corridor, with Clara's voice raised in a high whine. "Of course you can't see her, she's much too upset."

A man began to say something, but shrill protestations from Clara drowned him out. Harriet strode to the door and flung it open. A short, fattish middle-aged man was revealed with an untidy little moustache and mild brown eyes, like a sleepy hamster. His speech came in short bursts, as if the effort tired him.

"Inspector Bagshaw. Beckley CID. Sorry about all this. Can I have a word?"

"Of course," said Harriet. "Come on in."

His tone was not deliberately offensive. Perhaps he was too unfamiliar with the proper forms to address Harriet by her title.

As he came into the room Celia started up. "I'll go."

"No, please," said Harriet. "Do stay."

Celia subsided again, fighting down the butterflies in her stomach. She was outside her own police area and would not be recognised. But the old fear of involvement with the force still rose within her. Bagshaw's sleepy expression struck her as a mask to trap the unwary.

Clara had followed him into the room, and was mounting guard protectively over Harriet. Celia wondered if the protection would have been so formidable if Inspector Bagshaw had been female.

Invited to sit, Bagshaw uttered short phrases of condolence. They sounded tired, and had probably been used to survivors of miscellaneous tragedies several times a week for years.

"Thank you, you're very kind," Harriet murmured. "Can you tell me exactly what happened? I don't know anything except that my husband is dead."

He spoke gently. "Sorry. This is awful for you. Down in the river. In the reeds by the bank. Severe injuries to the head."

"But you don't know what caused them?"

"Violence of some kind. Try to fix the time of death, can we? When did he leave the house?"

"Early. When I woke up at seven, he'd gone."

"Often went out early, did he?"

"Not as a rule, but for the past few days he's been out every morning by then."

"Enjoying the fine summer weather?"

"Yes, or he may have wanted to do some odd jobs out there before he got caught up in the business of the day."

"No. No gardening tools with him."

"Would he have?" Harriet asked. "You say he was found in the river?"

"Yes. Wasn't killed there, though. Dragged there afterwards. There's a kind of shrubbery nearby. That's where he was attacked. Obvious signs of a struggle. Right in among the bushes, without even a pair of secateurs. What was he doing there? Any ideas?"

"No," said Harriet. Celia stirred uneasily in her seat but said nothing.

"Breakfast before he went out?" Bagshaw asked.

"Oh no. I began to be alarmed when he wasn't here to have it with me at half-past eight."

"Anyone else about the place as early as that?"

Harriet explained that the guides and cleaning women came in by the day, but never before nine. But the two gardeners started work at half-past eight.

"Could have come in earlier, though?"

"I suppose so, yes."

"No one else about in the grounds early? As far as you know?"

"No."

"Harriet, there was someone," Clara blurted out suddenly.

"Oh. Who?"

"Jack Martindale. I saw him from my bedroom window as I was dressing."

Harriet suppressed a gasp, as if this revelation shocked her.

"What time was that?" Bagshaw asked.

Clara hesitated. "About a quarter to eight."

"Where was he?"

"Crossing the lawn outside there, towards the stables."

"But Clara," said Harriet, staring at her, "what on earth would he be doing there at that hour?"

"How should I know?" answered Clara coldly.

Bagshaw's sleepy-looking eyes travelled from her to Harriet. "Let me know, will you, if you find out the answer? Leave you in peace now. We're questioning your staff. And the gardeners. Got a list from your Mr Glenville. Have to keep people out of the garden for a bit. Open the house to the public if you like."

At this Harriet started up. "Goodness, look at the time!

The rooms are still locked up and alarmed and Charles isn't here. I'll have to attend to it." She excused herself hastily and darted from the room.

Put out by her abrupt departure, Bagshaw looked after her, his expression no longer sleepy. "Will she be long?"

"I'm not sure."

Left alone with him, Celia wondered whether to go. But a question was nagging her. In the end she could not resist putting it to him. "Inspector, while you're waiting. You say Lord Clandon was killed in a shrubbery. Where exactly is it?"

His answer confirmed what she already suspected. He was describing one of the cornus beds.

"Then I think I know what he was doing there." She explained about the switching of the plant labels. "It happened twice, I know because I helped him put it right. If the practical joker did the same thing again, Lord Clandon probably went out to switch the labels back before anyone saw."

"Wanted to keep it to himself, did he? Why?"

"I'm not sure. But he said he knew who was doing it, and he didn't want a public fuss."

He thought for a moment. "Labels put back on the wrong bushes again? That why he was there?"

"Perhaps."

The brown eyes were suddenly alert as an idea struck him. Celia knew what was coming, but stayed resolutely silent.

"Expert, aren't you? You'd know. Helped him put it right before."

"Yes."

"Come down there with me, would you? See if the labels are wrong now."

This was perilously near to getting involved, but she could hardly refuse and followed him meekly out of the house.

49

By now the news of the murder was out and the media, frustrated by the locked door in the grand entrance portico, had discovered that all the comings and goings were taking place through the basement door in the stable yard. They crowded round Bagshaw as he came out, shouting questions and brandishing microphones and cameras. Celia, sheltering behind his considerable bulk, admired the calm platitudes with which he answered them without telling them anything at all. She was particularly grateful to him for limiting himself to a non-committal grunt when they asked him who she was.

A police cordon prevented them from pursuing their quarry down the garden. Trotting along beside Bagshaw, Celia forced herself not to ask the obvious questions: the nature of the injuries, whether the weapon had been found and so on. Instead, she asked whether he had a garden of his own.

The suggestion seemed to horrify him. "Not me! Live in a flat in the middle of Beckley."

Suddenly Celia understood. He was an asthmatic. By always keeping to short sentences, he could disguise his breathlessness when he had an attack.

"Interesting, what you said just now. Deceased thought he knew who the joker was that switched the labels."

"Yes."

"Didn't say who he had in mind?"

"No, but if I tell you who I think he suspected, will you please not take it too seriously?"

"With murder everything's serious at the start."

"Well, I'm pretty sure this isn't."

"Don't worry, tell me. Nightmare if we get the wrong man. We hate it."

But Celia was well aware of the other police nightmare: of not getting one's quota of convictions, to satisfy the political and financial pressures on the force. Reluctantly, she described Susan's arrival with her boyfriend in the rubber dinghy, and gave a slightly censored version of her conversation with them. "The opinions Lady Susan expressed were very green. She criticised her father's garden as unnatural and artificial, and condemned his use of chemicals. It occurred to me that she might have interfered with the plant labels to annoy him, as a kind of tease."

"Deceased had the same idea? Think so?"

"Yes."

"Made rude remarks to you, did they? Tried to frighten you away, so they could switch the labels on the bushes again?"

"Possibly. But of course, that doesn't mean that they murdered her father."

"No. Have to question them, though."

They had reached the river bank. "Landed from a boat, you said."

"That's right. An inflatable rubber one."

"Where?"

"Somewhere around here, I think. They tied it to an overhanging tree."

"That one?"

"Yes, I think so."

Further along the bank police and men in white overalls were everywhere, and roped-off areas were being minutely searched. A shape covered with a stretcher lay on the path ahead. She was grateful when Bagshaw skirted round it on another path to spare her sensibilities.

They were met by his team-mate, Detective Sergeant Simpson, a lanky man in his forties who was possessed of the normal powers of speech. "If you'll just come this way, Madam, I'll show you the area we're concerned with."

He led her to one of the cornus beds which had a small tent erected in the middle of it.

Bagshaw addressed one of the detectives standing by. "Roberts, exhibit. Let's have it here."

His telegraphic style seemed to have a secondary

51

purpose. It made his subordinates keep their wits about them.

Roberts handed him a plant label, holding it by its earth-covered spike to preserve any fingerprints. "Now. This the correct label for that bush?"

Roberts had lifted the flap of the tent. She looked in. The light sandy soil inside had been trampled. A half-grown cornus was looking battered, with several of the branches broken off. "Fell on it when he was attacked, we think," said Bagshaw, but refrained from pointing out the obvious: that the dark splashes on the large white flowers were made by blood.

"Well?" he asked. "You're the expert."

"This is not the right label. It belongs to *Cornus glabrata*, which is over there to your left. The specimen in there is a hybrid called Eddie's White Wonder."

"Good. Have a look round, d'you mind? Many others been swapped?"

She made a brief examination. "About half of them."

"I see. Must have been attacked half-way through putting it right. Any idea how long it would take him?"

"Let me see. I helped him with it twice. With both of us working, it took fifteen to twenty minutes."

"Good. Very much obliged to you. Thanks." He looked round, and called a uniformed policeman. "Constable Walsh. Escort the lady back to the house. Don't let the media up there trample her to death."

On the way Constable Walsh confessed himself a dedicated gardener, and explained his method of producing the giant onions and leeks and dahlias which won him prizes at all the local flower shows. But as they approached the stable yard she ceased to listen and panicked. The media were still swarming there like wasps. She would be photographed, asked who she was. She had left her all-concealing headscarf and dark glasses in the car. If there was a photo an informed newspaper reader who would know at once which Mrs Grant she was.

52

For a moment she considered asking Constable Walsh to find a blanket somewere and usher her to her car with it over her head, like a newly-arrested criminal. But to her relief a diversion made all precautions needless. A minibus with several children in it drove into the yard. Simon, back from playschool, got out. Before he could run into the house the media pounced and made him pose for them. Next morning, there would be a photo of the tragically bereaved four-year-old Fifteenth Earl of Clandon on every front page in the land.

The play school teacher got out of the minibus and took his hand. He looked up at her, wondering what was wrong, as she led him into the house.

Celia's heart bled for Harriet Clandon. Nobody could help her through the next agonising hour or two.

Inspector Alan Bagshaw and his team-mate Sergeant Chris Simpson watched Celia and her escort retreating uphill towards the house. For the moment, with the meticulous search for clues going on all round them, they had nothing much else to do.

"Queer little midget, isn't she?" Bagshaw commented. "A sort of ladylike Barbie Doll that's past its sell-by date. Don't trust her, though."

"Why not, Alan?"

"Tough. Tight little mouth. She was holding something back."

"She seemed quite straightforward to me," Simpson protested. He spent much of his time discouraging his superior from relying too heavily on his hunches about people. He also acted as interpreter when Bagshaw's utterances became too oracular for comfort.

"Funny family up there, Chris," Bagshaw mused. "Built themselves a bloody great house. Did anything else? Admirals? Generals? Statesmen?"

"Not that I know of."

"Useless lot, then."

"What's she like? The widow?"

"Not the screechy sort of countess. Doesn't have a voice like a demented carving knife. Cosy little woman, I'd say, when she's not in shock. There's a stepdaughter that's a horror, though. Shouted at me. Said there was a man in the garden first thing that shouldn't have been, name of Martindale. When she said it, the countess's eyebrows went right through the roof. Gave a great gasp too."

"She didn't believe it?"

"Or she suspected earthy goings-on. Could be that, if it's the same Martindale. The tomcat one that lost that paternity suit."

"Did you get a timing for him being seen?"

"A quarter to eight, she said. Come on, Chris, let's do some sums. The earl's out of the house by seven, right? Fiddled about with the labels. Then got attacked half-way through. Where does that get us?"

"It took the two of them fifteen to twenty minutes to put things right," Simpson reasoned. "Double that if there was only one, then halve it again because he was only half-way through when he was killed. Add on five minutes for him to walk down here from the house. That brings us out around twenty-five past seven."

Down by the river bank, one of the constables searching the site inch by inch shouted. "They found something?" murmured Bagshaw, and went over to look.

It was a long-handled sledgehammer hidden under a bush. After it had been photographed where it lay, it was eased gently on to a plastic sheet. It was a seven-pound one, of the sort used for knocking in fencing posts and tree stakes.

"Blood," said Bagshaw, peering at it. "Hair, Doc, come and look at this."

"I think that's fragment of bone from the skull," diagnosed the police surgeon. "They'll check in the lab."

"Murder weapon anyway," Bagshaw commented.

"Roberts. Those gardeners still about? Find them and bring them here."

In due course the three gardeners arrived: a tall, very handsome blond one, a beefy young one with a red face, and an older man, dark and wiry. After Bagshaw had checked their names against the list in his notebook, he showed them the sledgehammer on its transparent sheet. "Any of you know where this came from?"

"Yes," said Garton immediately. "It's from our tool-shed. Look, there's C for Clandon done with a hot poker on the handle."

"When did any of you see it last?"

Silence. Then Watts spoke. "It's been missing for a bit."

Garton looked at him sharply, but said nothing.

"Since when?" said Bagshaw.

Watts pondered. "I looked for it last week to knock in a stake in that new plantation, and it weren't there. You remember, Harry. On the Wednesday."

"No, that was the day I was weeding in the white garden. You should of told me Kevin, you know how hot he is, or was rather, on tools going missing."

"How about you?" Bagshaw asked the third gardener, who had said nothing. "You know it was missing?"

"I'm not on the staff here. I'm Mrs Grant's head gardener, here to do a job."

When they had gone, Bagshaw said: "What about it? Kevin?"

"It could be him. He gives the boss a bash with it, then loses his cool and chucks it in the bushes. Then he has to say it's been missing for days, but Garton doesn't back him up. But if it was Watts, we need a motive."

"Say it isn't him. Why didn't Garton back him up? What's his bloody motive?"

The meticulous search of the site continued for another hour before Bagshaw called it off, satisfied that nothing had been missed. On the way back to the cars, they passed

Harry Garton, doing some desultory weeding in a bed near the house. It was well past the magic hour of twelve, when all self-respecting gardeners knock off for lunch. He was loitering with intent.

As Bagshaw went past he sidled up to him. "I got something I oughter tell you. But don't say it was me you got it from."

"Let's have it, then."

"Young Kevin's got a girl into trouble. The boss said he was for the sack unless he married her." Harry put a sly finger to his nose. "Kevin's got a temper, and he hated the boss. You need to have a good look at him."

"Nasty slimy little serpent," Bagshaw commented. "Where does he think he is? The Garden of Eden?"

At Archerscroft Celia attended to urgent business, swallowed a hasty sandwich and prepared to go back to Winthrop. On top of coping with the police, the press and the funeral arrangements, Harriet would have on her hands a small boy devastated by the death of his father. She would need help, as soon as possible.

Bill misinterpreted the reasons for her hurried preparations, and treated her to one of his scoldings. "Now Celia. Why d'you want to rush off there and help the police with their enquiries? You always want to put your nose in where it don't belong."

"I keep telling you, I've no intention of getting involved."

"Okay but promise me you'll be back here tomorrow first thing. I dunno why you told her you'd go."

"She and that poor little boy are all alone in that huge house, except for the housekeeper and a half-mad stepdaughter straight out of a horror film. And the most awful people keep popping in, a weasely estate manager who's in disgrace with his family, and a very nosy travel agent whom she obviously hates."

"Name of Martindale."

"That's right. How d'you know?"

"The lads was talking about him in the pub. There's one of them says Lady Clandon had a go with him before she married the earl."

"Really? Does he know what he's talking about?"

"I doubt it." He repeated Harry Garton's fanciful version of events, including the appearance of the angry Mrs Martindale in the village schoolroom, brandishing the future Lady Clandon's nightdress in front of the delighted children.

"This sounds to me like a lot of highly coloured rubbish," Celia commented.

"I know, Harry Garton's a proper gossiping liar. But there might be some truth behind it."

"No. Strait-laced Clandon would never have married a fallen woman."

"Oh Celia, when it's sex you never know what they'll do."

"By the time they're sixty, they begin to simmer down."

"Not always. Suppose his hormones was on the rampage and he couldn't help himself."

"If you're an earl, there's no shortage of well brought up girls to cater for your hormones."

"Anyway, it's no business of yours. Concentrate on something serious. Does she still want that bed planted out? Find out when you get to Winthrop."

"She may be too upset still to think about it."

"You must make her decide. We got to know whether we're going to have four thousand African marigolds left on our hands or not."

"Horrors yes, I'll try."

When she went back to her cottage to pack, she realised that to look after and, if possible, amuse Simon was probably the most useful thing she could do when she arrived at Winthrop. Mounting to her attic she sorted out a miscellaneous collection of small toys which only

57

her weak-kneed sentimentality had saved from a trip to the dustbin. They dated from the upbringing of her own children, and had already been outgrown by grandchildren banished to far-flung parts of the world because of their parents' occupations. Selecting items likely to amuse a four-year-old, she put them in holdall and set off.

At Winthrop, everything seemed to have returned to normal. The visitors' car park was full, tourists were coming and going, the grand entrance under the portico was open. The gaudily-painted police cars had gone from the stable yard. Only the remains of the media circus, and the policeman detailed to control them, remained as a reminder of the morning's events.

"Oh, thank goodness you've come, Madam," said Mrs Holland, letting her into the private wing. "Her ladyship's at her wits end, what with the police here and Master Simon very fretful and difficult."

Harriet was in the sitting room, with Simon on her lap, fidgeting and kicking and pulling at her hair. Facing her were Inspector Bagshaw and his sergeant, both looking very frustrated. Clara was also there, mounting a feminist guard to protect Harriet from the two men.

"Hullo Simon," said Celia, standing in the doorway. "I've got some things for you in this bag. Would you like to come and see what they are?"

"Yes, Simon, do," Harriet urged.

Simon thought about this, then climbed down from his mother's lap and took Celia's hand.

"He wouldn't come to me," complained Clara as Celia led him out.

She took him along to the housekeeper's room and put the holdall down on the floor. Squatting beside it she opened the zip. "Now. What have we got in here?"

Intrigued, he put his hand in and pulled out a glove puppet. It held his attention for several minutes, and when his interest began to flag, a monkey on a stick was produced, and made to hold a lively dialogue with the glove puppet. Toy after toy was brought out in turn, and a very simple jigsaw puzzle kept trouble at bay for quite a time. But his attention span was proving no longer than most children's. So far Celia's luck had held. But how long would it continue?

In the sitting room the two policemen had perked up, thinking that now perhaps they would get some sensible answers. But Harriet's hands were tightly clenched in her lap. Bradshaw saw at once that being relieved of her child had not made her any calmer. He had seen this many times before. After the numbness of the first shock wore off, nerves soon became raw and depression set in. But he had to get some facts out of her.

"Sorry to go on and on about this. Think, please. Anyone hate your husband enough to kill him?"

"Not really. Oh dear, yes, there is someone with a grudge, but . . . no, it seems too absurd."

"Let's have it. No harm done if we go into it and decide to throw it out."

Overcoming her scruples, Harriet told him that her husband had dismissed Peter Harding from his post as a guide, and why.

"I see. Violent sort of man, is he? With a grudge? The sort who might do a thing like this?"

"He made a very violent attack on Mrs Grant. He blamed her for providing us with the evidence we needed to sack him."

Bagshaw made her describe the savage way Harding had rocked Celia's car. "Unbalanced, is he? Mad?"

"Well, he's been getting steadily odder for months. Losing his job here seems to have been the last straw."

"Drugs?"

"Possibly. I wouldn't know."

Harding would have to be interviewed, and he made Harriet produce his address. Then he asked her about the switching of the plant labels in the cornus beds. But it turned out that she knew nothing about it.

59

He was surprised. "Really? Went out early every morning without telling you why?"

"I suppose he must have done."

"Some reason, is there, why he wouldn't have told you?"

Silence.

"He thought he knew who the joker was. So I hear."

She had gone very tense indeed.

"Thought it was a prank by your stepdaughter Susan, didn't he?"

Relieved of the need to point a stepmotherly finger at Susan, she relaxed a little. "It probably was her. She's very green-minded and disapproves of what's happening to the garden."

"But he didn't mention it to you?"

"No. As her stepmother I have a difficult relationship with her, Inspector, and he'd naturally keep anything from me that might make things worse."

"Have to question her. Can I have her address?"

As he was being given it, the first signs of trouble echoed from along the corridor.

In the housekeeper's room the holdall was empty. Simon examined Celia solemnly. "Are you old or young?"

"What do you think?"

"I don't know." He looked up at her silver-white hair. "Your hair's old, but the rest of you isn't."

"Let's say I'm middling."

A pause. "Mummy isn't old, is she?"

"No, she's a lot younger than I am."

"But Daddy was old. Old people die. That's why he fell in the river."

The tears came, then howls of anguish which echoed through the house.

In the sitting room Harriet stood up in a fever of distress. "Oh dear. Is there anything else you want to ask me, Inspector?"

"Not now. Come back later if we need to." There

60

was no point in prolonging the interview with her in her present state.

Harriet fled along the corridor and the two detectives withdrew to their car. "What's next, Alan?" Simpson asked.

"Harding."

Simpson nodded. "He's the obvious suspect."

"Yes. Gets the sack, behaves like an elephant with a belly-ache. Rocks cars. On drugs most likely."

Harding lived just outside Winthrop village, in a foursquare Victorian house with a neat gravelled drive and a well-kept garden. "Must have private means," said Bagshaw. "Couldn't keep this place going on what they pay their guides."

There was no answer to their ring. Simpson rang again but there was still no result. They went round to the back. No one was about.

Simpson peered into the cobwebby window of the garage. "His car's not here."

Across the lane from the house was a small bungalow. "Ask there," Bagshaw suggested. "See if they know where he is."

The front door of the bungalow had the desolate look of an entrance which is never used, so they went round to the back and found an elderly couple having their tea in the kitchen. Asked if they knew their neighbour's whereabouts, they confirmed that he was not around.

"Know when he left?" Bagshaw asked.

"This morning, earlyish," said the old man. "When I went out to let out the hens, his car was out in the drive, ready."

"What time?"

"Half-seven, quarter to eight."

Bagshaw leaned forward, very alert. "D'you know how long it had been there?"

"We didn't hear it come out of the garage."

The two detectives exchanged glances.

"When did he leave?"

"I dunno. But I do his garden for him, see? When I went over there nineish, the house was locked up and his car had gone."

"You don't know where he went?"

He considered. "I don't know for sure, but when he's not on duty at the big house, he usually goes over to his mother's."

The old lady nodded approvingly. "To look after her. She's bedridden, poor thing."

"Know where his mother lives?"

They looked at each other. "He didn't tell us."

"Didn't leave you an address or phone number? In case of a break-in while he was away?"

"No. Funny, he never did."

"No other family that you know of?"

"No. He lives alone now. His wife left him."

"He used to hit her," said the old lady pityingly.

As they drove away, Simpson said: "I know what this is about. Bunbury. I'm sure that's it."

"Bunbury."

"That's what I said."

"Chris, I'm bad at crossword clues. Who or what the hell is Bunbury?"

"He's a person in a play by Oscar Wilde. My daughter was in it, they do theatricals in the village hall. There's a young man in it who's always having to go away to look after his friend Bunbury, who keeps falling ill. It turns out in the end that there's no such person, he's invented Bunbury as an excuse, to get away and avoid doing things that bore him."

Bagshaw let out a high pitched cackle of laughter. "Hard luck on old mother Bunbury. Doesn't get her pillow smoothed. Doesn't even exist, poor woman. What does sonny-boy get up to instead?"

"It's usually bigamy, two wives in different places."

"Not in this case. Some other variety of high jinks."

"Seriously, Alan," said Simpson. "His car was out in the drive at half-past seven. How long had it been out? Had it been to the big house and back?"

Bagshaw's moustache twitched. "Could be. Fun and games with a sledgehammer when he got there?"

Chapter Four

"Suspicious, Harding running off like that," said Simpson. "But we can't put out an Anxious to Interview yet, can we?"

"No," Bagshaw growled. "Look damn silly, won't we, if he turns up with a load of shopping from the supermarket."

"Bloody long shopping expedition," said Simpson. "He was away before nine, and its after five."

"Day at the races, then. What now? Back to headquarters? No. Kevin Watts. Lives this end of the village somewhere. See if there's anything in what that snake Garton told us."

Kevin's home was in a row of Victorian workers' cottages. He was in the back garden, earthing up potatoes. Asked to state his whereabouts early that morning he leant on his spade, thought about it, and said: "I went round me rabbit snares."

"Get any?" Bagshaw asked.

"One. Mum's cooking it now."

"Where did you get it?"

Kevin grinned sheepishly but did not answer.

"Come on now. We're not gamekeepers. In the park at Winthrop, was it?"

He nodded cagily.

"Whereabouts in the park?"

"Hanger Wood."

"Where's that?

"Top of the ridge, this side of the river."

"See into the garden from there, could you?"

"Nah, cos I was in the wood."

Bagshaw paused. "Anyone there with you?"

"Nah."

"Anyone see you come back?"

"Me mum, when I give her the rabbit." Horror dawned slowly on his face. "You don't think it was me who bashed him?"

"Didn't like him, did you?" said Bagshaw.

The look of horror deepened. "He's okay. No worse than most bosses, I reckon."

"How about your girlfriend and her baby? He was on at you to marry her. So they say."

"She's not my girlfriend. Who told you about that?"

"Never you mind. Came and lectured you about it, did he?"

"Nah." Kevin frowned. "He come and talked to me mum, though."

"Let's have a word with her, then."

"Sure." He went to the back door of the cottage and said something in a low voice. After a few moment his mother came out, wiping her hands on her apron. Her enormous bulk suggested that Kevin's tendency to put on weight was due to an inherited gene.

She launched into a tirade at once. "That's right, what Kevin says. His Lordship did come snooping around and making nasty remarks about our Kevin's Christian duty. I told the old fool straight, I did. This is nothing to do with you, I said, and nothing to do with Kevin either. That little slut's opened her legs to all the boys for miles around. God knows who its father is, I says, and the sooner it's got rid of the better. But His Lordship has a fit of the horrors when I say she should get rid of it, and then he says, all holy and sorrowful, 'But she told the vicar the dear little child was Kevin's.' Well, I mean to say, who in their senses tells the vicar the gospel truth? Our Kevin's not going to marry that rubbishy bit of goods and that's flat, and if His Lordship don't like it he can stuff it."

She had not lowered her voice. Gardens up and down the row of cottages had filled with spectators, and arguments developed across the dividing fences over the rights and wrongs of her strictures on the young woman. The two detectives withdrew from the scene to take stock.

Bagshaw grinned. "Gave the old fool a flea in the ear. According to her. Think she's telling the truth?"

"Near enough. If Clandon had threatened to sack her Kevin she'd have come out with it."

"So why did Harry Garton shop him? What's he playing at?"

There was no obvious answer.

They drove back into Beckley. But as Simpson slowed down to turn in to police headquarters Bagshaw suddenly said "No".

"Where then, Alan?"

"Martindale, before he shuts shop."

Fairsquare Travel occupied two smallish first floor rooms in the main street of Beckley. The outer office contained a middle-aged secretary whose blonde locks with their dark parting owed nothing to nature. Shown into Jack Martindale's sanctum, Bagshaw viewed its over-scented, over-handsome occupant with distaste. Had he really been at Winthrop early that morning? He seemed too ornamental, too elegantly dressed to commit murder, or perhaps too busy there seducing one of the maids.

He greeted the two detectives with lamentations about the loss of his dear friend and valued client Charley Clandon. "And poor little Harriet, she'll be lost without him."

Bagshaw let this run its course, then said that as a matter of routine he was asking everyone connected with the case to account for their movements between five-thirty and eight that morning.

"Needless to say, I was in bed, Inspector."

"Sure? Not in the garden at Winthrop? They say you were seen there a bit before eight."

Martindale sat up sharply. "Who on earth told you that?"

"Information received."

Martindale plunged into thought. "Not Harriet, she's too honest. I know, it was Clara, getting her own back. She's half-mad, had a letch for me and I turned her down. Of course I wasn't there. I tell you, I was in bed."

"Anyone able to confirm this?"

"Actually, I wasn't at home." He smiled, showing too many beautiful teeth. "We three are men of the world, aren't we?"

Disgusted, Bagshaw put on a men-of-the-world expression. "If you'll just tell us the lady's name. In confidence, of course."

Simpson's pencil was poised over his notebook.

"Oh," said Martindale. "I'll have to ask her permission first."

"You do that. We'll be back," Bagshaw promised.

Back at the car he summed up sourly. "Splendid. Gives himself time to decide which of his floozies to parade for our benefit. Tell her what to say, too."

"You think he was at Winthrop then, up to no good?"

"Probably not. Lady Clara sounded furious with him. Could have told a naughty fib. We keep him on hold while we chase up Harding."

They had had a long day, and Chris Simpson felt it was time to knock off. But Bagshaw was still full of energy. "The green couple. What were they doing, fiddling those name tags? Better go there and find out."

They ran Susan Winthrop and her boyfriend to earth in the basement flat of a multiple-occupation house in a run-down part of the town. The door was opened by a well-built young man with a two-day growth of beard.

67

"Well, well, Ron Fisher," said Bagshaw, not unkindly. "Fancy running into you again."

"Hullo, Mr Bagshaw," said Ron cheerfully. "How come you're here? You got nothing on me, I'm clean."

Susan Winthrop appeared behind him in the doorway. "Ronald is as pure as the driven snow," she insisted. "And when I say snow I mean what happens in winter, not the prohibited substance you disapprove of."

"You meet a nasty class of person where I been," Ron complained. "Thass why I been going straight ever since I came out." He smiled charmingly. "So fuck off, why don't you?"

"I do think," said Susan, "that as Ronald puts it so elegantly, you should leave. You have no right to persecute a man who has paid his debt to what is laughingly known as society."

Ron made a sudden attempt to shut the detectives out. But Simpson had his foot in the door.

"If you were more sensitive," said Susan, as Ron stamped on Simpson's foot, "you would realise that you are not exactly welcome."

"Try to be sensible, shall we?" said Bradshaw comfortably. "You're not what I came for, Ron. Bad news for Susan, I'm afraid."

"Lady Susan to you, Inspector," she retorted.

"I'm sorry, I'm sure," said Bagshaw mildly. "You haven't listened to any news broadcasts today, Lady Susan?"

"No. We don't, it's all lies anyway. What's happened?"

"Sorry to say, your father's been killed."

"Oh," she said in a flat, shocked tone. "What happened, a car smash?"

"No. Found in the river this morning. Severe injuries to the head."

"You mean, someone did him?" Ron asked.

"Must have."

"That's nasty," said Susan. "He wasn't my favourite man, not since my bloody stepmother made him turn Winthrop into a fun fair. But I don't approve."

"Nor do we," Bagshaw murmured. "Puzzled about one or two things, though. Come in and talk to you for a moment?"

The pair consulted each other mutely.

"We don't know nothing," said Ron.

Susan held the door open. "Come in and see where we lead our squalid underprivileged lives."

Apart from a scattering of cassettes and magazines, the only evidence of squalor in the pleasantly furnished bed-sitting room was the unmade bed. The detectives sat down and Simpson got out his notebook.

"Last week," Bagshaw began. "In a rubber dinghy, weren't you? Little building in the garden at Winthrop. Went in, didn't you?"

"Wass he on about?" Ron enquired.

"We understand," Simpson interpreted, "that on the morning of May the twenty-eighth you and Mr Fisher landed from a rubber dinghy in the garden of Winthrop Court, and entered a building known as the Temple of Flora."

She turned to Ron. "Did we?"

Ron shrugged. "I got a bad memory."

"You did," said Bagshaw mildly. "Information received."

"Yes, and I know who told you," said Susan pertly. "It was that haughty little lady who crept up behind us, oozing refinement and white-haired elegance. Did she also tell you we intended to go in there and have what is politely known as sex?"

"She says that was what you told her, but she didn't believe it."

"How astute of her, she was quite right. I only said that to scare her off."

"What did you really intend to do in the building?"

"I'm afraid that's a secret."

"Making mysteries? Why?"

"Because I want to."

"Now Lady Susan, don't be silly – madam."

His sarcastic intonation on the "madam" was not lost on her. "I'm not telling you," she shouted in a fury. "There's a key to the temple in Busyboots Glenville's office over the stables. If you want to know what we were up to in there, you can bloody well go and borrow it and have a look."

"No way," Bagshaw retorted without raising his voice. "If you're going to play silly buggers I'll have to treat you rough."

"Why not tell him?" Ron suggested. "He's nasty when he gets rough."

"You're right Ronald dear, one should humour unstable people with dangerous delusions. The truth is, Inspector, that we were preparing a surprise for my father. Ron and I have been painting a fresco in there for his birthday."

"A fresco? Subject?"

"It's not pornographic, if that's what you were hoping."

Bagshaw waved this aside with contempt. "Something green? To tease your father."

"To make him see the error of his ways," she corrected.

"Why scare Mrs Grant off?"

"She was so small and creepy and upper-class, a sort of scaled down Madame de Pompadour. She got on my nerves."

"Another reason, wasn't there? The plant labels. Didn't want her to see what you were up to."

"What plant labels?" she asked scornfully.

Simpson intervened again. "The inspector is suggesting that you didn't want Mrs Grant to see you changing around the labels of some of the bushes in that part of the garden."

She stiffened. "I don't understand. What is all this?"

"For the past week or so," Simpson went on, "someone

has been pulling up the labels from bushes in the shrubbery down by the river, and sticking them in the ground again by the wrong bushes."

The pair looked at each other in amazement, as if at a loss.

"Another green joke to tease your father?" Bagshaw suggested.

"Of course not, I wouldn't dream of doing such a thing. Conserving rare species is about the only activity of his that doesn't stick in my environmental gullet."

"Hold on," Ron interrupted. "Why are you grilling us about this?"

"Your dad was putting the labels back right when he was killed."

There was a tense, shocked silence, which lasted for over a minute before Fisher broke it. "You bastard."

"You dirty cheating buggers," hissed Susan.

"Trying to frame us, that's it," Ron shouted. "Just because I got done for that load of Ecstasy."

"Which you pigs planted on him," added Susan.

"What's all this panic?" asked Bagshaw, surprised. "No one's saying you killed him. Anyone could have."

To calm them further, Simpson added: "We're perfectly prepared to accept that you moved the labels as an innocent prank."

"Why aren't you perfectly prepared to accept that we did nothing of the kind?" snapped Susan.

"Who else would have?" Bagshaw countered. "They say your dad was sure it was you."

"My father is widely known in the county to be stark staring mad."

"Was," corrected Bagshaw calmly.

"I beg your pardon?"

"'Was widely known' not 'is'."

"Very well, but the usual diagnosis is religious mania induced by the superstitious practices of the Church of England."

71

Frustrated, Bagshaw tried another tack. "Now, don't have hysterics. We'll ask everyone this. Only a matter of form. What were your movements between say five-thirty and eight this morning?"

"Any movements we made were in bed, Inspector."

"No one to confirm that, I suppose?"

"No one, alas. Voyeurs tend to concentrate on basements, and we've had trouble that way. So when we're making movements, as you call it, we keep the curtains drawn."

"And last night. You got home when?"

They consulted each other silently.

"Early," said Ron.

"We ate at home," added Susan, "and stayed up late, watching a deliciously tacky horror film on the telly."

"No visitors during the evening?"

"No, Inspector," said Susan.

"Tut, tut," Ron lamented. "We should have got some drug baron to fix us up with a dodgy alibi."

Susan shot a venomous look at Bagshaw. "We haven't done anything wrong, and we have no alibi. But you need to earn your performance-related pay by getting your quota of convictions, so go away and dream up a miscarriage of justice against us."

"Oh, what nonsense," sighed Bagshaw.

"Go," said Susan, every inch an earl's daughter. "You make me vomit, get out before I throw up all over you. Ronald, show them out."

He took them to the door. Away from Susan, he became much less sure of himself. "We've not done anything wrong. Honest, we haven't," he murmured as he let them out.

As the two detectives drove away, Simpson said: "What d'you reckon? Was that just left-wing prejudice against the police, or were they holding out on us?"

"Scared, Chris. Its natural. We barge in on a murder rap and he has form."

"He was a small-time pusher, wasn't he?" said Simpson. "Just to feed his own addiction. But why did they deny interfering with those labels?"

"Deny everything on principle, that sort do."

"Hold on though, Alan. Say they came there to interfere with the labels again, and he found them at it."

"No. Been interfered with already. He was putting them right."

"Then they came to carry on with their painting, and he spotted them and there was a quarrel."

"Could be," said Bagshaw. "Fisher's known to be violent."

"You mean that stabbing. We suspected him, but it was never proven."

"Rave party the night before? Did it because they were high on this and that?"

"Yes, and Clandon says something nasty to the girl, and Fisher blows his top. Was there a rave party anywhere last night, Alan? We better find out."

They drove for a time in silence.

"Could he have got hold of that hammer from the tool shed?" Simpson asked.

"Anyone could. You don't lock tool sheds in the daytime."

"But if it's that, Alan, he took it some days earlier, when it went missing. He planned to kill Clandon, so we can forget about rave parties and last-minute quarrels."

"That's right," said Bagshaw and fell silent again.

After a time Simpson said: "You having one of your hunches, Alan?"

"Hunches? No. Puzzled, yes."

In the private sitting room at Winthrop Celia was teaching Simon to pay Snap, while Harriet grappled with the business of bereavement in the business room. The ormoulu clock on the mantelpiece showed ten to six.

73

The last tour of the house had ended, and the public car park was almost empty.

The door opened and Harriet came into the room with George Glenville in hot pursuit. "Please, Harriet," he argued, "do let me take this chore off you."

"Thanks, George, but no. I used to lock up when Charles was away. From now on it's my job for good."

"But you've had a very stressful day. I'll attend to it, just this once."

"No," Harriet repeated, slightly on edge. "I'm doing it myself tonight, and Simon's going to help me, aren't you, love?"

Simon looked up from the card table and nodded solemnly. "Cos Daddy can't. He's dead."

"I mean it, George." She softened slightly. "But thanks anyway."

He went, and Harriet gave Celia a conspiratorial smile of relief. "Right," she said. "Let's start the routine."

But when she opened the door at the end of the corridor and led the way out into the Great Hall, a far from routine spectacle confronted her. All the guides and restaurant staff had assembled there under the dome, with the pensioner who manned the ticket desk as their spokesman.

"We wanted to let you know, my lady, how sorry we all are. But we carried on like you said, His Lordship would have wished it, and we would like to assure you that we shall do everything we can to support you in your task of continuing his work here."

Murmurs of agreement followed, and Simon, standing dolefully beside Harriet, was sympathised with as a "poor little mite". Harriet, barely controlling tears, said: "Oh thank you, Mr Finch. Thank you all." She managed to rise to the occasion with a few more suitable phrases, but was able to break off when Finch handed her the cash box containing the day's takings.

74

Harriet took it and handed it to Simon. "Put it in the business room, love, will you?"

Simon went, looking solemn and important. The staff filed out through the massive front door and Harriet locked and bolted it behind them.

"Will you really carry on as before, like they said?" Celia asked.

"Of course. And he was mad keen on that flowerbed of yours, so do get on with it as soon as you can."

"We will when things have settled down a bit," said Celia.

When the locks on the windows of the Great Hall had been checked, Harriet led them into the dining room. In the middle of the table was the massive silver-gilt object given to the Sixth Earl by the Empress Catherine the Great.

"Was he really one of her lovers?" Celia asked.

"No. Did that ass Harding say he was?"

"He implied it."

Harriet laughed. "No, visiting ambassadors weren't considered virile enough. Catherine fancied very tall footmen and soldiers, people like that. She had a tumble with one most mornings before breakfast, after a lady in waiting had tried him out and passed him as a satisfactory performer. Anyway, this thing has to be put in the safe overnight in case a burglar takes a shine to it."

With an effort, she picked the massive object up. Followed by Celia and Simon, she carried it through to the business room in the private wing. "Now, Simon love. These are Daddy's keys, and this is the one that opens his desk. See if you can unlock it."

With a little help, Simon managed to unlock the old-fashioned roll-top desk. Harriet rolled back the top. "Now look in that little drawer, and you'll find the key of the safe. Yes, that's it."

The key was big, and the lock of the old-fashioned safe stiff, but Simon got it open. The Augsburg table centre was stowed inside it, along with the cash box containing the day's takings. The key was put back in the little drawer, and the desk locked.

The next task was to make the range of state rooms secure for the night. While the house was being shown, each door had been locked by the guide after he had taken his group through it into the next room. The same procedure had to be followed now. In addition, window catches had to be checked, and massive shutters closed.

The master key had been entrusted to Simon, who was happily unlocking and locking doors. When they came to the bedrooms Harriet murmured: "Keep Simon here for a moment while I go on ahead."

Celia managed to hold him in conversation till Harriet reappeared in the passage. "Sorry about that," she explained in an undertone, "but a dodge you have to watch out for is someone hiding till the house is locked up. So one has to look under the beds and in the wardrobes. But if Simon had seen me looking under all the four posters for bogeymen, he'd have had nightmares."

When the rooms upstairs had been dealt with, they went back to the business room. Harriet opened a wall cupboard, revealing the push-button panels of a formidable security system.

"Can I?" begged Simon.

"No, love, if you got it wrong we'd have the place surrounded by police cars in ten minutes."

She punched in the combinations to set the alarms for different parts of the building, but left one panel untouched. "That one covers the private wing, so I don't set it till we go to bed. The security lights outside come on automatically if there's anyone out there after dark."

When everything had been attended to, Harriet took Simon upstairs to bath him and put him to bed, leaving Celia to go into the sitting room and help herself to a drink. She found Clara there, hidden behind a newspaper with a large gin and tonic beside her. She lowered the

76

newspaper when Celia had poured herself a stiff whisky, and prepared for conversation.

"I suppose I must get something black to wear at the funeral. D'you think I should?"

"Not unless you want to."

"But the media will be there."

"Even so, anything low-key would do. Black isn't considered essential any more as a mark of sorrow."

"It is in Houston, Texas," said Clara gloomily. "I had to drape myself in crepe from head to foot for Edward and Jessica."

Harriet read Simon a story and got him to sleep. Supper, cooked and served by Mrs Holland, was eaten and the household retired for an early night. Celia nodded off at once, and was in a deep sleep when she began to have a nightmare. But it was not her usual one, to the effect that she was a pot-bound saxifrage whom no one would report. This time she was being repotted very savagely by someone with no consideration for her feelings. Someone, possibly herself, was making a terrible noise, a sort of warbling scream.

She woke, to find Harriet shaking her violently by the shoulder. "We're being burgled," she whispered.

Celia sat up in bed. It was pitch dark. "Are you sure?"

"Yes. Listen."

She realised now that the warbling noise in her dream had not stopped when she woke. The burglar alarm was making a hideous outcry.

"I was reading in bed because I couldn't sleep," said Harriet, "and my bedside light went off. None of the lights switch on, the current's been cut at the main."

"The alarm still rings with the electricity cut off?"

"Yes. There's a standby battery."

"Will it still alert the police?"

"Yes. They're on their way. I've just phoned them to make doubly sure."

"They haven't cut the phone then?"

"We've always kept a cellphone by the bed. It's one of the standard precautions."

Someone with a flashlight was standing in the open doorway. "Oh, my lady, there you are!"

"It's all right, Mrs Holland," said Harriet. "The police are on their way."

"I was so frightened when I saw you weren't in your room. I was afraid you'd gone downstairs."

"To do a macho act with Charles's shotgun? No thank you."

Outside the window headlight beams shot through the darkness of the park. Soon three police cars were lined up below, with their lights playing on the front of the house. Harriet threw up the window and shouted: "We're up here. Shall I come down and let you in?"

"No, madam. There's a window open where the intruders got in. Please stay where you are while we search the premises."

"Very well, but the rooms are all locked. If you wait a moment I'll throw you down the master key."

Taking Mrs Holland's flashlight she fetched a massive bunch of keys from her room, threaded a scarf through the key ring as a marker, and threw it down to the knot of uniformed policemen below.

While they waited for the house to be searched, Harriet gave a guilty start. "Clara. Where is she? Good heavens, I forgot all about her."

They hurried along the passage and knocked on the door of Clara's room. "Who's there?" asked a frightened voice from inside.

"Harriet." She tried the door and found it locked. "Do let me in."

The door opened. "Oh, You're alive, then," Clara remarked.

"Of course. Why shouldn't I be?"

"Someone hates our family. Which of us is going to be killed next?"

"No one at present, we're too busy being burgled. Oh dear, I wonder what they've taken. Not the Chelsea Physic Garden plates, I hope. I'm rather fond of those."

A powerful flashlight approached from the direction of the stairs, and a voice said: "Sergeant Thomson, madam, Hampshire Constablary. The intruders have left if you'd like to come down and see what's missing."

"Oh dear, is there much?" Harriet asked.

"Only the contents of the safe, as far as we can see, and whatever valuables there were in that desk."

Accompanied by Celia, Harriet followed Sergeant Thomson down the stairs and into the business room. He shone the flashlamp on the safe. The key was in the lock and it was empty. The Augsburg table centre had gone.

"The desk's a mess," said Sergeant Thomson, turning his flashlight on it.

This was no exaggeration. The roll-top had been prised open brutally, and the contents of all the small drawers and pigeon-holes inside had been scattered. Of the larger drawers to either side of the kneehole, the two at the top, which had been locked, had been forced, so violently that the jemmy had splintered the wood, and their contents had been dumped on the floor. Seeing this, Harriet choked back a little cry of distress.

"Was there something valuable in there?" Thomson asked.

"No, only the key of the safe," said Harriet in a shocked voice. "Its the violence that upsets me."

"Which drawer was the key in?"

Without speaking, Harriet pointed to the drawer which had been forced on the right hand side of the kneehole.

"They knew the key was in the desk," Thomson reasoned. "But they didn't know where. They broke open the roll-top, but it wasn't there. So they forced more drawers till they found it."

"Yes. That must be it," said Harriet in a voice high

with strain. Sensing that she was near to breaking point, Celia suggested that she should go back to bed and leave further investigation till the morning.

She agreed. Escorted by Thomson with his flashlamp, they started up the staircase. But half-way up Harriet swayed and leant heavily on Celia's arm. "Sorry, I'm feeling a bit giddy. I'll have to sit down."

She sat on one of the steps and put her head between her knees. Celia borrowed the flashlamp and fetched her a glass of water from the kitchen, and she soon began to recover. "Silly of me to have the vapours," she remarked. "But what with Charles being killed and now this, it's all been a bit much."

Dawn was breaking. Celia settled her down in bed, then went back to her own room. But she could not sleep. Something had happened which she could not understand. Asked whereabouts in the desk the key had been kept, Harriet had pointed to the big drawer to the right of the kneehole. But Celia had been there when she locked up the safe, and put the key in one of the small drawers inside the roll-top.

Chapter Five

By nine next morning Winthrop Court was swarming with police activity. The grounds were being searched for clues. Fingerprints were being taken everywhere, including those of Harriet, Celia and Mrs Holland. When Harriet's had been taken she asked if it would be all right for her to fetch something from the business room.

It was not. Forensics were still crawling all over it in a vain search for clues.

"What is it you want?" asked Bagshaw. "Fetch it for you."

"Very well. In the top drawer of the filing cabinet beside the desk, you'll find a lot of folders containing photographs. Could you bring me the folder marked 'Dining Room'?"

"You photograph everything for insurance?" Celia asked as they waited.

"All the pictures, and everything else that might be stolen. If something goes you need ever so many copies of the photo, the police and the salerooms and the press all want one."

When Bagshaw produced the file, she spread out the contents on a console table. The photos of the items in the dining room were all in separate envelopes. She opened the one marked 'Augsburg Table Centre' and took out a dozen pictures of it.

She handed one to Bagshaw. "Here you are Inspector. That's for your records."

He thanked her, and excused himself. The superintendent from the regional CID had arrived. With him was Chief Inspector Weaver of the arts squad, the specialist unit responsible for investigating art thefts from country houses.

"What's that you've got there?" said Weaver when they met Bagshaw in the Great Hall.

"Photo of the thing they stole, sir."

"They took *that*!" said Weaver, sounding incredulous.

"Yes, sir."

"Well, well. Has Lady Clandon any more copies of this photo? If so, she can give them to me and I'll distribute them to the press and the arts magazines and the sale rooms for her."

When Bagshaw had briefed his two superiors on progress to date, Weaver looked gloomy. "Oh dear, a state of the art security system, and a safe dating from the dark ages that opens with a key. Will they never learn?"

He and the superintendent withdrew to their car for consultation. "There's one thing we must decide at once, Geoffrey," the superintendent remarked.

"You mean, are we dealing with one crime or two?"

"Exactly. It's your pigeon if Clandon was killed because he'd discovered somehow that the big boys had got Winthrop in their sights. But if he was killed for some quite different reason, and our villains came along a few hours later with their own independent agenda, there are two separate pigeons."

Weaver nodded. "And one of them's mine and the other is Bagshaw's."

"What d'you think? Is the timing a coincidence?"

"Not necessarily, even if the two things are separate. Whoever did this knew there'd been a murder. They reckoned the household would be in disarray, with no fear of being met by an angry member of the House of Lords armed with a shotgun. It's the obvious moment to attack."

"Would art thieves really rub out Clandon just before they struck?" the superintendent objected. "If someone's got wind of your plans, you don't kill him, you fade away quietly and set up an operation at some other house."

"I agree. All the respectable practitioners have a horror of violence. But the people who did this weren't respectable practitioners, they were ignorant cowboys."

"You're sure, Geoffrey?"

"Yes. Remember all that porcelain in the glass cases in the corridor? Shelf after shelf of it. Even the rarest pieces aren't unique, the factory always turned them out in batches. No need to explain to the buyer where your copy came from. That Kändler monkey orchestra alone is worth well over a million. But the ignorant oafs leave the porcelain, and steal a unique Ludkens *surtout de table* with Augsburg assay stamps all over it, that's illustrated in all the books on continental silver. The chances of selling a thing like that are absolutely nil."

"It couldn't have been stolen to order?"

"Not unless you believe the fairy-tales about a mad collector gloating over a hoard of stolen masterpieces that he daren't show to anyone."

"They could be hoping for a ransom," suggested the superintendent.

"Who'd pay? A ransom's simply an invitation to go and steal something else. The insurance companies know that, even if these idiots don't."

"But they knew that silver-gilt thingamy was in the safe. They knew the key to the safe was kept in the desk. Someone inside told them. You'll want to find out who. But all the people in your sights for that will also be in Bagshaw's sights as possible murder suspects, he's got one or two in the frame already. If we had the same cast of characters being interviewed by two different lots of detectives, it would be a nightmare of crossed wires. D'you want to take over the whole thing from Bagshaw?"

Weaver hesitated. "How effective is he?"

"Well, he looks a bit sleepy. But don't let that put you off, he's quite bright. There's obviously a local angle to this, and he knows the local scene. I'd be quite happy to leave him in charge, but it's your decision."

"I'd say no if one of the big international gangs was involved. But as it's just cowboys making a mess of things, I'm happy to leave it to him and provide any input he needs from us."

"Okay then, let's have him over and tell him."

Summoned by the superintendent's driver, Bagshaw came out of the house and down the front steps at a comfortable amble and joined them in the car.

"We've got two crimes here that may be interconnected," the superintendent began. "And we don't want a lot of muddle and duplication, with two investigations overlapping."

"No, sir."

"So we think you should be in charge of them both."

"Very well, sir." Only a twitch of the untidy moustache betrayed his surprise at not having the case taken over by high-powered specialists.

Weaver gave him a thorough briefing, dealing mainly with the use he could make of regional resources if he needed them. "And while you're investigating possible murder suspects, you can also examine the background of everyone who knew where the key to that safe was kept. Some of them will be the same people, no doubt."

In the presence of his superiors, Bagshaw made an effort to be coherent. He confessed that he had already had a chat with Lady Clandon, who said that two elderly tourists had been seen behaving suspiciously in the house ten days earlier, and that their descriptions had been reported to a voluntary organisation dealing with security at country houses where valuables were kept.

"Good," said Weaver. "You can ask Ripley to tip you the wink if this couple turn up elsewhere."

"Puzzled by one point about them though, sir. They

were on a spying mission, ready for a future break-in. Stole a vase though, Lady Clandon says. Why steal and draw attention to themselves? Risk raising the alarm? You'd think they wouldn't."

"Professional art thieves wouldn't," said Weaver. "But as I told you, these people are cowboys."

After a pause, Bagshaw said: "Anything more, gentlemen? No? Then I'd better get back in the house."

His two superiors were about to drive off when a detective constable from the regional squad came hurrying out towards them.

Weaver lowered the window. "Yes, Williams?"

"It's about that lady that's a house guest here. It's Mrs Grant."

"Oh? What about her?"

"Mrs Grant of Archerscroft Nurseries, sir. I recognised her from when I was stationed at Welstead. I'm sure it's her."

"Oh. That Mrs Grant."

"Yes sir. And I thought—"

"You thought quite right Williams, well done. We'll have a word with her." He turned to the superintendent. "You don't remember? But for her a bunch of green maniacs would have wrecked the Chelsea Flower Show. Lawson at Welstead thinks the world of her, she'd have done well in the CID."

"And she's a friend of the family here? A stroke of luck for Bagshaw."

"Let's butter her up a bit before we pass her on to him. Give her lunch?"

Back in the house, Bagshaw had sought out Lady Clandon. "Were you proposing to open the house to tourists today?"

"No, thank goodness. Wednesday is one of the days we stay shut."

He too was thankful for this. His men were still searching the house and grounds for clues.

"Will you need me any more, Inspector?" Celia asked him.

"No madam. Got your address if there's anything."

Harriet began begging her to stay, but was interrupted by the arrival of George Glenville, carring a small parccl.

"I bought something that I think might cheer up poor little Simon," he said.

Harriet did not look particularly grateful. "If you're in to lunch you can give it him then."

"He's not here?"

"No. He's at playschool."

"You sent him?"

"He said he wanted to go."

"I see," said Glenville in a voice which suggested that he did not approve.

When he had gone, Harriet said: "What impertinence! I don't know what business it is of his."

Half-way across the stable yard to her car, Celia was intercepted by a tall figure, resplendent in a senior police officer's uniform.

"Mrs Grant?" said Chief Inspector Weaver.

"Yes."

"The legendary Mrs Grant of Chelsea Flower Show fame?"

"Horrors. I did ask everyone to keep very quiet about that."

"I know, but policemen are the most frightful gossips. The superintendent and I were hoping you could spare time to have lunch with us."

No, not on your nelly, Celia decided. "I'm sorry. I was away from the office for most of yesterday. I must get back there and catch up."

"Oh dear. We would very much like to have a word with you."

"Then perhaps we could have it now."

"It's a bit public here," he objected.

Knowing that she would have to let them have their say, she remembered that there was a lay-by half-way along the Beckley by-pass. She arranged to meet them there, and get it over.

The superintendent's sleek Jaguar followed her closely all the way to the rendezvous. *In case I try to give them the slip,* she thought grimly.

Once in the lay-by, and cossetted in the leather upholstery of the Jaguar, she listened to a great deal of flattery, then said firmly that she was determined not to get involved in the investigation.

"Oh, why not, Mrs Grant? Up to now, you've always been very helpful, and you know the people involved."

"That's the point. Lady Clandon's a friend of mine. I'm not prepared to spy on her and her household and report the results to Inspector Bagshaw."

"It's not exactly spying, is it?" urged the superintendent. "You were a witness when two very serious crimes were committed, and you're a very observant and reliable witness. You have a duty."

"I've a duty as a witness, yes. But detection isn't my job, and in this case there will be all sorts of hair-raising complications if I get involved in it. Please don't press me."

The two men exchanged looks, and the superintendent gave Weaver a barely perceptible nod, as if to say: Go ahead, pull out all the stops, even some very dishonest ones if you have to.

"Mrs Grant, can we consider what this crime is about?" Weaver began.

"It's about a man being murdered, after which a pretentious and ridiculously valuable object was stolen," she replied.

"Oh no, Mrs Grant, it's about much more than that."

"More than murder?"

"Yes. We're talking about mass murder."

He paused to let this sink in. "Have you ever wondered

why we take art thefts from country houses so seriously? No? Perhaps you don't realise what an effort we're making over this case. Inspector Bagshaw's working flat out at the local end, and I've got twenty men standing by to follow up any lead we get to the international gang that's probably behind this heist. I agree with you: that thing being stolen is no more important in the long run than a hundred other crimes that were committed in the south of England last night. What is important is the people who stole it, and what they'll do next. They probably stole it because they had a buyer lined up, and when they get the money they'll take it straight to Amsterdam, and put the proceeds into one of the big drug syndicates. Between them the syndicates control huge sums in laundered money, probably as much as the budget of the European Community, and they use it to corrupt whole governments and sap at the very foundations of society. This is why we take these art thefts so seriously. Think about it, Mrs Grant. In my book anyone who buys into a drug syndicate is a mass murderer."

Celia said nothing, but felt trapped.

"So can I tell Inspector Bagshaw to get in touch with you?"

"Oh dear. I suppose so, yes."

When she had driven off, Weaver said complacently: "That was naughty of me, but it did the trick."

Speeding away towards Archerscroft, Celia decided that she would have to talk to Inspector Bagshaw after all. But she was determined not to tell him that Harriet had lied to him about which desk drawer she had put the key in.

Bagshaw, meanwhile, had left Sergeant Simpson to look after the investigation in the business room and sauntered down the garden. He wanted to have a close look at the river bank, because one of the country house gangs had recently made a sensational escape with their loot by water. He was not overawed by being made responsible for investigating a major art theft, though nothing so specialised had come his way before. Making his way along the river bank, he reflected comfortably that one was never out of one's depth if one concentrated on asking the right questions.

Opposite the cornus beds he came to a halt. A mooring stake had been driven into the mud at the edge of the river and the reeds and nettles on the bank had been trampled. He thought back to the last time he had been here, with the scene-of-crime team after Lord Clandon's murder. If the stake had been there then, they could not possibly have missed it. It was new.

He looked carefully for signs that the sharp prow of a boat had been driven into the bank, but there were none. But he arranged for the area round the stake to be photographed, and set uniformed policemen crawling about on the bank looking for clues. Closer examination of disturbance among the reeds suggested that the boat had been round-headed. Like a rubber dinghy, he decided, and that started a train of thought. Susan Winthrop and Ron Fisher had come and gone in a rubber dinghy. He looked along the bank at the little garden temple in the wood, which had been the scene of their activities.

What had they really been up to in there? He had better see.

He tried the heavy door, but it was locked. According to Lady Susan, there was a key in the estate office over the stables. He made his way back there, and climbed the stairs to Glenville's office.

"Oh, you mean the Temple of Flora," said Glenville when he was clear which building Bagshaw meant. He went over to a panel on the wall where rows of keys hung on hooks. "I'm afraid it isn't here."

"Know who has it?"

"Sorry, no. Now that I come to think of it, it's been missing for some time."

"Would there be any objection, d'you think, if we picked the lock?"

"I'm sure Lady Clandon wouldn't mind, but I don't know what you'll find in there."

Accompanied by Simpson and Detective Constable Luckhurst, who had the necessary tools and expertise, he went back to the Temple of Flora. The lock yielded easily, as if it had recently been oiled. The three policemen went in and found an empty room with a stone seat along the wall facing the door.

"Cor, look at that!"

"Blimey."

"Nasty, I call it."

The fresco which faced them on the wall space above the seat depicted a naked man in full frontal view, with exaggeratedly large genitals. He was vaguely recognisable as a caricature of Lord Clandon. Arrows transfixing various parts of his anatomy had labels attached, each bearing the name of a chemical and the toxic effect it was alleged to have on the human frame.

"To persuade her father not to use chemicals in the garden," Bagshaw commented.

Tubes of paint and other artists' materials were neatly stacked under the stone seat. Some brushes were in a jam jar, soaking in white spirit. The tubular metal brush case in which they belonged lay beside it.

Bagshaw opened it, expecting to find more brushes. There were none. Instead he pulled out a small plastic bag, transparent and neatly closured, containing pills of some kind.

"Ecstasy?" Simpson queried.

"I think so, yes," said Bagshaw. "Enough to keep a whole rave party happy."

No action could be taken about this discovery till the contents of the plastic bag had been analysed in the police laboratory. Bagshaw's next task was to find out from Lady Clandon which members of the staff were likely to know that the key to the safe was kept in her husband's desk in the business room. Unfortunately she could give no clear answer. She had hardly ever been present while he was closing up the public part of the house, and was not sure exactly what routine he followed. It was possible that some of the people who manned the ticket desk brought the cash box to him in the business room, and on at least one occasion the guide doing the last tour had brought him the table centre to put in the safe. Bagshaw resigned himself to examining the backgrounds of all the people who worked in the house.

"One more question, may I?" he said. "The key to the safe. Last night. Put it in the drawer to the right of the kneehole, is that right?"

"Yes, Inspector."

"That where your husband always put it?"

"I'm not sure. He may have put it in different places from time to time as a precaution."

"Ah. They knew the key was in the desk, not which drawer. Someone on the staff saw him do that, tipped them off. Someone that hovered around in there several times, to see where he put it. Who? Harding?"

"Possibly," said Harriet. "He rather liked coming into the private wing when he got a chance. But that was because he had a silly crush on me. It could have been any of them."

Harding was still absent. A constable sent to his house had found no one there. He might well have known the whereabouts of the key to the safe, and he was also a potential murder suspect. He clearly suffered from some mania, whether drug-induced or not. After his violent attack on Mrs Grant it was quite likely that he had turned on Lord Clandon, as the person ultimately responsible for sacking him from his job as a guide.

Unable to exclude other possibilities, Bagshaw set in train the machinery for checking the bona fides of a score of middle-aged village ladies and retired gentlemen who worked in the house. Nothing was found more serious than a caution for speeding and two parking fines. For good measure, he also had the outdoor staff investigated, including Harry Garton. He had no criminal record. But he was a regular user of cannabis, with occasional orgies on Ecstasy. He was not, as far as the entry on the computer showed, a pusher. In accordance with established policy in such cases, a blind eye had been turned and he had merely been cautioned. According to the record, he was a bachelor living alone, with no known income apart from his wages, which could hardly run to buying Ecstasy except as an occasional treat.

Back at Winthrop, Bagshaw found Garton weeding the long border. As a drug user, he might be responsible for the find in the Temple of Flora, so he asked him if he had ever been in there.

"No, sir, it's kept locked."

"D'you know where there's a key?"

"It would be up at the house, sir, in the estate office."

"No, it's missing from there."

"Then I know who's got it. Lady Susan and her boy friend."

Was that the only key? Bagshaw wondered. If so, the Ecstasy must belong to Ron or Susan.

"And I know what those two got up to in there," Garton added with a grin.

Had he managed to sneak a look at the fresco? Evidently not, to judge from his next remark.

"Well, it stands to reason, doesn't it, sir? Locking herself up in there with a strapping young fellow like that."

Enough of this nonsense, Bagshaw thought. "You smoke cannabis, don't you?" he said sternly. "And that's not the only thing you get high on."

"No sir, it's a lie. I never touch anything like that now, not since the police had a word with me and I saw the error of me ways."

But his eyes showed that he was frightened.

92

Visited by a vague flash of intuition, Bagshaw asked: "D'you know Peter Harding at all?"

To his surprise mere fright was replaced by a glint of pure terror, quickly concealed. "Him that works up at the house? Or did."

"That's right."

"I may have spoken to him once or twice in the pub, nothing more."

There was clearly a great deal more, and Bagshaw pressed him to reveal it. But he had recovered enough composure to deny that he knew Harding at all well, and made haste to change the subject. "His Lordship being killed like that was a great shock to us all," he blurted out. "He was a wonderful employer, popular with all of us, except – did you talk to young Watts, like I said, that had a grudge against His Lordship?"

"Yes, and there's no evidence whatever that Lord Clandon threatened to sack him."

Garton's mention of Watts had clearly been a diversionary tactic, to get away from the awkward subject of his relationship with Harding. Sounding as ominous as possible, Bagshaw said he would be wanting to talk to him again later, and turned to go.

What was the key to this mysterious relationship? Drugs, possibly, with Garton as the customer and Harding as the pusher. But where did Garton get the money? In due course there would have to be a search for prohibited substances at his cottage.

It was late afternoon, and there was still no sign of Harding. It began to look as if he was in hiding, in which case a public appeal to him to come forward might well drive him into even deeper hiding. Bagshaw decided to apply for a warrant to search his house, in the hope that some clue to his whereabouts might be found there. To get it from a reluctant authority he had to exaggerate a little and depict Harding's attack on Mrs Grant as the act of a blood-crazed would-be murderer. This did the trick.

Armed with the warrant, he took a team of searchers to the house.

The elderly couple living opposite had no key, and Detective Constable Luckhurst, the specialist in such matters, had to exercise his talents on the lock. The interior was obsessively tidy, with all signs of human habitation removed or put away in cupboards. There was nothing in the pockets of the three suits in the wardrobe, and the chest of drawers contained only shirts, socks and underclothes. Only the contents of the refrigerator suggested unfinished business, in the shape of half-eaten portions of food.

"Hey, Luckhurst, have a go at this," said Simpson.

The drawer of a small table with a telephone on it was locked, but soon yielded to Luckhurst's delicate attentions. It contained the local directory and a pop-up device containing telephone numbers, with an alphabetical easy-reference index.

Bagshaw gave a grunt of satisfaction. "Now let's see."

Harding had noted down remarkably few numbers, mostly of local shops and services, with one or two private addresses in and around the village. But on one of the pages they found a seven digit number, in the London area to judge from the code, with no name against it. The only clue to the number's owner was the fact that Harding had entered it under the letter H.

There were similar entries under L, O, R, S and W, all with codes in or around London. But under S there were two entries, with initials beside them to remind Harding which was which: SM was presumably Smith or Smithson, and there were various possibilities for ST.

"Undercover contacts of some kind," Bagshaw commented. "We'll fax them to regional. Weaver can get someone in London to chase them up."

Leaving everything in the house looking undisturbed, Bagshaw sent Simpson to chase up the laboratory report on the prohibited substance found in the Temple of Flora, and went himself to the premises of a voluntary organisation dealing with the resettlement of ex-prisoners, to find out what it knew about Ron Fisher. The report was favourable. After getting over his heroin addiction, he had been transferred to an open prison where he had applied himself seriously to training as a carpenter and cabinet-maker. So far as the organisation knew, he was now in regular employment, and in a stable relationship with a young woman. In short, a successful case of rehabilitation, of a kind which unfortunately was all too rare.

Bagshaw would have been more ready to take this optimistic assessment at its face value if Simpson had not joined him for an early evening pint at the pub, and told him that according to the laboratory the quantity of Ecstasy found in the Temple of Flora was enough to suggest wholesale salesmanship rather than personal use.

By now, Fisher would be home from work. Taking Simpson with him, he drove to the basement flat, intending to conduct a fierce interview. But on the way he changed his mind. "Going to play this gently. Don't be surprised," he told Simpson as he rang the bell.

It was Susan who answered the door. "Well, what can I do for you this time?"

"One or two points," he began. "May we come in?"

"Yes. Quickly, before anyone sees you." She hurried them into the flat. "I've been doorstepped by reporters all day. Whoever told them I was living here deserves a lethal dose of something very unenvironmental. It wasn't you, by any chance?"

"Me? Not guilty."

"Ronald's only just got home, he's in the bath. If you want to quiz him about his lurid past you'll have to wait."

Bagshaw ignored this. "We saw your fresco. Full of arrows, your dad."

"Witchcraft, did you think? With the arrows sticking into him because the wall was too hard to take pins?" After a moment's silence she added: "If you did, you're wrong. I was very fond of him really, only I wished he wouldn't be so wrong-headed. I'm dreadfully sorry he's dead."

She knows we've been in there to look at the painting, Bagshaw reasoned, so she knows we must have searched the place. Why is she so calm? Doesn't she know the cache of Ecstasy was there? Was it a bit of private enterprise by Ron?

Presently Ron emerged from the bathroom wearing nothing but a towel round his middle and an impressive array of muscles. When he saw the two detectives he greeted them with a sulky frown. "What, you lot again?"

"The inspector's been saying how much he admired father, all stuck with arrows like Saint Sebastian."

The frown lifted and was replaced by a grin. "Oh yeah. It was who Susie did most of it. The lettering's mine, though."

He sounded relaxed, but Bagshaw was not convinced. When arrested for possession of Ecstasy, he had shown himself a very convincing liar.

"How long did the whole thing take you?" Bagshaw asked.

Ron began putting on a shirt. "Oh, two-three weekends. It was for Susie's dad's birthday, that's not till next month, but we wanted to finish because I got next week off and we was going down to Devon. But we can't now, not with the funeral and all."

"You were there a week before Lord Clandon was killed," said Bagshaw. "That was when you put the final touches?"

"That's right," Susan agreed. "We meant to take away the brushes and so on, but we couldn't because of Madame de Pompadour."

Bagshaw looked puzzled.

"You know, the classy lady who crept up behind us in

96

the wood. She was parading round the garden like a traffic warden, and if she saw us coming out of there with a lot of painting materials, she would have told father and spoilt the surprise."

"But the painting isn't what you came to quiz us about?" Susan queried.

"No. The key to the temple. There was one at the Winthrop estate office, you said. I was wondering. It's missing. You got it?"

"No. I crept in there one day when Eager-Beaver Glenville was busy being the great executive somewhere else, and snitched the key to have it copied. I put it back a few days later."

Was she lying? By insisting that there was another key, they were establishing that anything incriminating found in the temple could have been planted there by someone else, and nothing to do with them.

"Bother!" exclaimed Susan. "So when I told Father to look at his birthday present, which he'd find in the Temple of Flora, he wouldn't have been able to get in." She saddened. "Not that it matters now."

"So how did you get in?" Ron asked.

Bagshaw winked. "We have our methods."

"I bet you bloody have."

"One other thing." said Bagshaw. "The plant labels. Must have been you. No one else would. Don't see why you won't admit it."

Suddenly the atmosphere was very tense.

"We won't admit it because we didn't do it," snapped Susan.

"Thass right," growled Ron.

"This isn't the Middle Ages," Susan shouted in a fury, "so you can't torture us till we confess to something we didn't do. So why don't you fuck off and let me get Ron his supper?"

"Because I'm not finished. I'll need to take a look at that rubber dinghy of yours."

"You can't," said Susan.

"Why not?"

"We've sold it."

"You've *what?*"

"We sold it. It was cluttering up the place, and with the painting finished we didn't need it any more."

"Who did you sell it to?" Bagshaw demanded.

Ron gave a self-satisfied smirk. "Dunno. A guy we met at a boot sale."

"Description?"

"Can't remember."

"Start remembering bloody quick if you want to stay out of trouble."

"Whoy?"

"We want it back. Forensic examination."

"Whoy? Whass all this?"

"Burglars used a boat like that for their getaway. May have used it for the murder too. Sold yours, so you say. Didn't want forensics to give it a once-over."

"Thank God we did," Susan screamed. "If we hadn't you'd have smeared it with blood from Father's corpse and stitched us up for killing him."

Ron was squaring up for a violent attack on Bradshaw, but Susan checked him. "Don't. He'd have you for assaulting a police officer. Get out, you two, or I won't be responsible for what happens."

With an effort, Ron refrained from assaulting them. But he hustled them out, like a nightclub bouncer dispatching drunks who had misbehaved, into the arms of the media who had been attracted to the scene by the sight of Bradshaw's car parked outside the house. Their ignominious expulsion prompted a fever of speculation among the journalists, who brandished microphones and shouted questions. Glum-faced, they fought their way through to the car.

"They'll put that on the telly tonight," prophesied

Simpson gloomily as they drove away, "and we'll look damn silly."

Bagshaw grunted. "Sillier if we'd stopped and let them film us chatting them up."

After they had gone a little distance, he said: "Well, Chris, what did you make of all that?"

"You didn't ask them about the Ecstasy."

"No. Wouldn't have been any the wiser. They'd say we planted it."

"Relaxed, weren't they? As if they didn't know it was there."

"Susan didn't. He may have. He's clever, very street-wise."

Back at headquarters a report from forensics was waiting on Bagshaw's desk. Two sets of prints had been found on the plant labels, those of the deceased and Mrs Grant. But on top of both sets there were traces which suggested that someone had handled the labels wearing gloves.

"Who would wear gloves?" asked Simpson. "Not those two."

"No. They'd be suspected, with or without."

"Is someone trying to frame them, then? Switching the plant labels and planting the Ecstasy? There was another key to the temple."

"So they say, Chris."

"That could be true, and it's gone missing. Someone has it."

Bagshaw frowned. "What about them selling the boat, though?"

"That makes them either very innocent or very guilty."

Chapter Six

Celia lay awake for a long time, with warring emotions churning around in her head. She was haunted by Chief Inspector Weaver's lurid account of the international background to the Winthrop burglary. Anything to do with drugs horrified her, and his picture of drug money being laundered on a massive scale and used to subvert governments was terrifying. Her public duty was clear. She must give what help she could to Inspector Bagshaw.

But she also had a private duty of loyalty to a friend. She shrank from the prospect of spying on Harriet Clandon, who seemed to have chosen her to lean on in the distress of bereavement and the shock of being burgled. Harriet had deceived the police, there was no getting round that. Asked where in the desk she had put the key of the safe that night, she had told them a deliberate lie. Why? It was tantalising. Curiosity, Celia's besetting sin, was gnawing at her, she had to find out.

But Bagshaw must be kept out of it. Any suggestion that Harriet had something to hide would bring him down on her like a ton of accusing bricks. Anyway, how could it be relevant? Harriet could have nothing to do with international drug traffickers who stole art treasures and laundered money and had probably murdered her husband.

Next day it was business as usual, beginning with her morning conference with Bill in the office. He strode in from the frame yard looking grumpy.

"Must I go over to Winthrop and carry on? There's lots to do here."

"I told you, she wants it finished as soon as possible. As a sort of memorial to her husband, I suppose. And it's a bit of an eyesore half-done like that, with the garden open to the public."

"Then I better get over there now."

"Yes. I'll collect the first batch of bedding plants from that place in Basingstoke and join you there."

"Why? We're not ready to plant them out yet."

"They say we must take delivery now, and we don't want a lot of vulgar French marigolds lowering the tone here. I can dump them in the working area at Winthrop."

"Oh Celia, I see what it is. Winthrop's crawling with policemen after the burglary, and you're dead set to get over there and muck in."

"No, damn you!" she cried. Then conscience struck, for she disliked lying to Bill. "As a matter of fact they've pressurised me. They say stealing art treasures is linked up with international drug trafficking and all sorts of horrors, and it's my duty to do what I can."

"Oh Celia, I don't believe a word of that, they've conned you. Try not to neglect the business too much, that's all. See you later."

He drove off in what seemed to be a huff, but he was smiling secretly as soon as he was outside the gate. He was fond of Celia, and knew that she got bored with the business from time to time and needed some outlet for her surplus energy. It alarmed him when the outlet took the form of messing with violent crime, because it often exposed her to danger. But he knew that when something like this happened she was like a warhorse pawing the ground, and nothing he could say would stop her.

At Winthrop he found that Kevin Watts had gone on barrowing compost on to the new bed, but there was no sign of Garton. "Hi Kevin. Where's Harry?"

101

"Off sick."

"How come?"

"Someone beat him up last night."

"They did? What for?"

Kevin emptied his barrow-load on to the bed. "Harry makes enemies."

"Is that right? How?"

"Too fond of sticking his dirty nose in other people's business."

"Anyone's business in particular?"

"Nah. Everyone's. He's got sex on the brain, see? Other people's sex. He's frustrated, on account of he's got no girlfriend."

"You mean, he's a Peeping Tom? Something like that?"

"Well, you heard him sounding off the other day."

Bill was disgusted. "I call that a feeble way of getting your kicks."

"Sright. Give me a nice lively bit of ass any day." Kevin turned the barrow to refill it from the trailer. "He'll be back working tomorrow, he says. Don't let on to him that I told you."

Celia, meanwhile, was running behind schedule. After dealing with routine morning chores at Archerscroft, she called at the wholesaler's from whom she had ordered the bedding plants. Maddeningly, her consignment was not ready, and she had to hang around for half an hour while it was assembled and the paper-work made up. As a result it was half-past eleven by the time she arrived at Winthrop.

The stable yard was already thronged with paying sightseers as she drove through it and on into the screened-off working area with cold frames and sheds for tools and machinery. Bill and Kevin were there with the garden tractor and trailer, which they were about to fill with another load of compost and earth. She made them off-load her bedding plants, then went with them to the site to inspect and approve their morning's work.

By then twelve had struck. Bill and Kevin prepared to leave for the pub, but Celia hung back.

"You're not eating with us?" Bill queried.

She explained that Harriet had phoned that morning to find out if she was coming over, and had invited her to lunch.

Bill grinned. "On the sniffer-dog trail?"

"No. Comforting the bereaved."

He made a disbelieving face and left her.

It was far too early to present herself at the house for lunch, so she treated herself to a stroll through the enclosures below the terrace, intending to walk back up the central vista and check, as she went, whether the new bed was going to be visible as one approached the steps. But near the bottom she turned off into one of the garden enclosures which she particularly liked. It was full of yellow spring flowering roses, Canary Bird and Ecae and Hugonis and her special favourite, Rosa Primula which filled the air with the scent of incense. She strolled in, and was startled to see Susan Winthrop already there, sitting reading on a stone seat.

Susan looked up. "Goodness, it's Madame de Pompadour!"

"Not really," said Celia. "I'm not cut out to be a royal mistress who bosses cabinet ministers about."

"You were bossy down there in the wood."

"Was I? I try not to be. If you're as small as I am, it looks ridiculous, as if I was the Queen of the Fairies in a tantrum."

Susan giggled. "To be fair, I don't think you were bossing us about. You just stood there looking elegant and composed. You made me feel like a fat schoolgirl of fourteen, and I said something naughty to shock you."

"Which I didn't believe."

"I wonder why not?"

103

"Garden temples are a bit chilly and damp for that sort of carry-on and I was sure you had other opportunities."

"We did have, but not any more for the present."

"Why not?"

"Oh, don't you know? The media were doorstepping us at the flat, and printing nasty little hints about Ronald. So Harriet invited us to stay here till things calm down."

"Oh, good. That was thoughtful of her."

"Yes, I was wrong about her. She's much nicer than I thought she was. But she says unless Ronald and I have separate bedrooms, Father will start doing somersaults in his vault."

"Where is Ron?" Celia asked.

"At work, he's a very high-class carpenter. At the weekend he's going to repair that desk that got smashed up in the burglary. Come on, let's go in. It's almost time for lunch."

On the way up to the house Susan said: "It's lovely being here where we're protected a bit from the media. But the police are still getting up my nose."

"Because you altered the labels in the cornus beds where your father was killed?"

"We didn't!" said Susan indignantly. "They keep insisting that we must have done, because it's the sort of thing we might quite easily be expected to do, but we really didn't, someone else must have. But I can't think why anyone would."

"Nor can I," said Celia, and fell into a thoughtful silence which lasted till they reached the house.

In the private sitting room, Harriet was kneeling on the floor playing a game with Simon. Clara, dissociating herself from this, sat staring out of the window with her back to the room. The arrival of Celia and Susan was the signal for pre-lunch drinks. But Harriet's nerves were on edge, and her hand with the sherry unsteady. "Sorry, d'you mind pouring?" she said, handing the decanter to Celia. "I had another session with that awful insurance man this morning. Anyone would think I'd slaughtered Charles and burgled the house myself."

While Celia poured drinks and tried to cheer Harriet up, Simon rushed round the room in an excited state, which turned to sulks when he found he was no longer the centre of attention. Predictably, this led to trouble during lunch, when he refused to eat his fishfingers and salad.

"But you like fishfingers!" wailed Harriet in distress. "You know you do!"

"No! Horrid fishfingers!" he shouted as she pushed a forkful at him.

A sensible mother would have recognised this behaviour as a bid for attention and ignored it. But that was too much to expect of Harriet in her bereaved and distraught state. While she went on cajoling him to eat, Celia looked round the table and realised that George Glenville was not in his usual place. She asked where he was.

Clara roused herself from her near-coma and explained: "George didn't approve of Susan and Ronald being invited to stay here. There was a row, and Harriet told him to go and eat somewhere else."

At intervals during lunch Celia had been brooding over the problem of the cornus beds, and at coffee time she managed to get Susan into a corner and return to the subject. "I know you didn't change those labels. But had you played that sort of trick before?"

Susan giggled. "Yes, just after Father opened the family fun-fair to the public in the spring. Ronald and I switched all the signposts around, so that men wanting a pee would be directed to the fern grotto, and people would trudge down to the river and look for the restaurant there."

"Did you do this more than once?"

"Yes, every night for a week. Father knew it was me, and was horribly embarrassed. He used to creep out and put it right in the early morning before everyone was up."

Celia was pleased. Here was a titbit of information that she could offer to Bagshaw without compromising with her principles.

Down in the village Bagshaw's men had their ears to the ground, and news of the attack on Harry Garton had reached him by midday. Who had attacked him? Peter Harding, with whom he seemed to have a mysterious connection? Anyway, the attack had better be investigated.

Taking Simpson with him, Bagshaw went to Garton's tumbledown old cottage. They found the victim slumped in an armchair in his kitchen. He was in a bad way, with an eye half-closed, five stitches in a scalp wound, and a mass of painful bruises elsewhere.

"Someone play nasty rough games with you, did they?" Bagshaw asked.

The only reply was a piteous groan.

"Harding, was it?"

Fright appeared in the eye that was not closed. "Nah."

"You sure? I bet it was."

"Nah."

"Know who it was then, do you?"

"Nah."

"How many of them were there?"

This seemed to need some thought. "Two."

"Last night, was it? On your way home from the Red Lion? Tennish?"

"Sright."

"Drunk and disorderly, were you? Had a skinful? Sure you weren't seeing double?"

"Nah. There was two."

"What sort of men? Tall? Short?"

"I dunno. Couldn't see."

"Go on. You must have."

It was getting on for midsummer, and it would still be quite light at ten when the Red Lion closed.

After some thought, Garton declared that his two attackers had been wearing balaclavas.

"Saw their balaclavas, did you? Then you know if they were tall or short."

A long pause for thought. "Middling."

"Clothes?"

"Trousers. Bomber jackets."

Bagshaw did not bother to ask what colour the clothes were; there was no point in playing this game any longer. He stood up. "Mind if we have a look round?"

Garton grunted something, but his expression was uneasy. There was probably a twist or two of cannabis somewhere in the place. If it could be found, real pressure could be put on him to tell the truth. Bagshaw watched him closely as Simpson went upstairs to search the bedroom. The uneasiness did not increase. Whatever was causing it was almost certainly here, in the kitchen.

Ranging round the room, Bagshaw searched a cupboard full of kitchen stores without provoking any change in Garton's resigned expression. But as he looked for other possible hiding places he watched Garton's face and saw that the barometer of unease rose sharply every time he passed the TV set. There was also a video recorder. Both were probably stolen.

"Bought them at a boot sale," said Garton comfortably when he stopped to examine them. Stolen goods bought in a casual market like a car boot sale could not be reclaimed by the original owners.

But Garton was still worried about something to do with the TV. What? There was a cassette in the recorder. Bagshaw pressed the eject button to release it. To judge from the title, it was hard porn.

There were two more cassettes of the same kind on a shelf above the set. Garton's face was a mixture of guilty fear and a kind of obscene glee. "Want to have a look-see?"

"You horny old goat, you make me puke," Bagshaw retorted.

How had he managed to pay for them? Hard porn did not come cheap. "Where did you get these?"

"Borrowed them from a friend."

"Friends? You don't have any."

Simpson appeared in the doorway. "Nothing upstairs."

Bagshaw showed him the cassettes.

"The usual," Simpson commented. "From that shop in Beckley."

Though Garton's shameful secret was now out in the open, Bagshaw noticed that he was still looking uneasy. There must be something else to find.

Watching Garton's reaction to his movements, he realised that this time the sensitive area was near the fireplace. Among oddments on the mantelshelf there was a rusty tobacco tin, which he opened. It contained five hundred pounds in fifty pound notes.

"Hey, that's me life savings," moaned Garton.

It was time to put the boot in. "You dirty little wanker," Bagshaw shouted, picking up the cassettes. "Been selling people drugs. Spend the money on filthy pictures to jerk yourself in front of."

Garton decided to have a spectacular breakdown of health. His paroxysm of coughing was so violent that it almost threw him out of his chair. When it was over he sat clutching his heart and groaning in agony. "You can see I'm not well," he gasped, choking. "I been beaten up and I got pains all over and me head aches something awful. You got no call to come shouting at me with nasty accusations while I'm ill."

"We'll go when you stop telling us fairy stories. Who was it beat you up?"

But it was no good pressing him. It only prompted him to make his symptoms more dramatic and noisy. They were unlikely for the moment to learn anything more, and if Garton decided to make trouble, the Police Complaints

Commission would take a poor view of detectives who bullied an alleged invalid. They withdrew, taking the cassettes with them and promising to return later.

On the way back to headquarters, where routine paperwork awaited them, Simpson suggested that it was time to contact the famous Mrs Grant.

"Hell no, why?" Bagshaw laughed. "Cross her hand with silver, shall I? Madame Grant, clairvoyant, with her sensational crystal ball."

"Regional were very keen on her," Simpson reminded him.

"Only because of all that hype from Lawson at Welstead. Wait for her to ring us, can't we?"

At regional headquarters Chief Inspector Weaver was in conference with the superintendent.

"Bagshaw has come up with something quite promising," he said as he handed over a list of names, addresses and telephone numbers.

The superintendent looked doubtful. "Why does he think this is worth following up?"

"Harding disappeared a few hours after Lord Clandon's murder."

"Then there's nothing to connect him with the break-in twelve hours later."

"Except that he's one of the people who could have known where the key of that safe was kept."

"And you think he was the inside man for an organised mob?"

"Bagshaw does."

"Why does he think these are the mob's addresses?"

"The phone numbers were found with no names against them in a locked drawer."

"So he wants us to have them all in for questioning?"

"No," said Weaver. "He's pretty sure Harding's got a second identity somewhere, probably under another name. If we alert them, they'll tell him we're on to him. He'll be off in a flash and Bagshaw will never find him."

"Does that matter? He's only the inside man, not the ringleader."

"Bagshaw wouldn't agree with you. He's got Harding in the frame for Clandon's murder. He wants us to organise surveillance, till one of them leads him to Harding."

"Does he indeed? On all six? That's tying up a lot of manpower. Besides, these people are cowboys, they're not in the big league."

"Organised mobs of cowboys can do a lot of damage. Let's face it, having six names is a lucky break. We don't know where it will lead us, but we must follow it up."

The superintendent made a discontented face. "I'm not having tails put on six dark horses, we haven't the manpower. Find out who they all are, and we'll pick the likeliest.

"Okay, I'll fix it and tell him."

"Has he been in touch with Mrs Grant yet?"

"I'm not sure. He seemed rather allergic to the idea. I'll check."

Bagshaw, meanwhile, was in conference with a man called Parker whom he had taken an instant dislike to. He was small and lean, with a buttoned-up mouth and eyes set too close together. He was acting for the insurers of the Winthrop treasures, and he was asking searching questions. "Inspector, would you say Lady Clandon seemed to you nervous?"

"She seemed upset, yes. You would be if you'd been burgled and had your husband killed."

"I meant nervous under questioning. I'm pretty sure she wasn't being straight with me. I think the Augsburg *dessus de table* is somewhere on the premises. But how can you search a barracks of a house that size?"

"An insurance scam, you think? All by herself? Enterprising little woman."

"What about that estate manager, name of Glenville?

Not too bad looking, and her husband was over sixty. How about him as her accomplice? He has his own key to that safe, but he'd have to break into the desk and get the other one. Otherwise it wouldn't look like a burglary from outside."

"But Mr Parker, that desk ended up a wreck, fit for the knackers yard. Why? She'd have told him which drawer to find the key in."

"I've thought about that, Inspector. She claims that her husband used to put the key in different places in the desk, as a precaution, but she was looking very seasick when she said it, and I don't think it's true. They could have decided that he'd better do a thorough job on the desk to make it seem more like an outside job by someone who didn't know where to look."

Bagshaw's suspicions were still concentrated on Harding. But he saw now that this theory had to be taken seriously.

"There's the time factor too," Parker went on. "In the nine minutes between the alarm going off and the squad cars arriving, the intruder, if there was one, had broken three locks on that desk, unlocked the safe, taken out the *dessus de table* and got clear away. But Glenville knew the code of the burglar alarm. He could have walked into the house, switched off the alarm, dealt with the desk and helped himself to that thing in the safe. Then he sets the alarm again, goes out and hides the loot in a safe place. All he has to do now is break in, trigger the alarm and walk out again. By the time the police arrive, he's in his rubber boat, floating away down the river."

"He's her lover then? Killed the earl so he could marry her?"

"I'm only concerned with the insurance aspect. Murder isn't in my province."

"Pretty lurid scenario, though," said Bagshaw. "Better tell you. We're following up another lead, very hot."

"Yes?"

"Various people with addresses in London have connections with a man the Clandons had just sacked."

"Ah. I'll note down the details if I may."

"No."

"Oh, please."

"No. I know you insurance people. Rush in to get there before we do, foul things up."

Parker went on arguing, and ended by uttering threats. His superiors would complain over Bagshaw's head that he was failing to co-operate. "God know how I kept my foot off his nasty little arse," Bagshaw told Simpson after more or less throwing Parker out.

When Chief Inspector Weaver received the report on Harding's undercover contacts, he showed it to the superintendent. "Well, it's a suitable mix of occupations, anyway. Four professionals to provide the brains, and two heavies for the dirty work."

The superintendent looked at the list. All six were men, four married and two single. Among them were a chartered accountant, an employee of one of the high street banks, and a dweller at a seedy address in Wandsworth who described himself as a company director. But there were also two building labourers and, unexpectedly, a dentist.

"Perhaps they only call him in when they need to drill a safe," Weaver suggested.

"Then let's count him out. Company directors and chartered accountants are always getting up to mischief, put a tail on those two and the bank clerk and forget the others."

Weaver gave his instructions. From then on the chartered accountant and the seedy company director would be followed wherever they went by a team of plain-clothes policemen working round the clock, till one of them betrayed their secret or led them to Harding.

The day came of Lord Clandon's funeral at All Saints' Church, Winthrop. A small detachment of uniformed constables was controlling the traffic and trying to prevent the funeral of the Fourteenth Earl of Clandon from degenerating into a media circus. In this they were not wholly successful. As the Earl was being laid to rest with his forefathers in the family vault, the photographers had run riot, clambering over tombstones and pushing the mourners aside. But having got their pictures, they made off, and the mourners were able to get out of the churchyard unmolested.

Presently a long procession of cars was winding its way up the village street and through the park towards Winthrop Court, to which the mourners, including all the estate employees, had been invited for refreshments. By the time Celia reached the house, having been pressed to come by Harriet, the gathering in the ballroom had abandoned the subdued tones thought proper at the start of such occasions, and was beginning to sound like a normally cheerful drinks party.

Harriet was receiving people as they arrived, with Simon standing beside her. "Bless you for coming, Celia," she murmured. "Stay on for a bit afterwards, won't you?"

"I'm sorry, I've got a date."

George Glenville was hovering nearby. "Harriet, Simon must be getting very bored. Let me take him away and get him something to eat." He looked down, smiling. "You'd like that, wouldn't you Simon?"

Simon smiled up at him and took his hand.

"D'you want to make him sick?" said Harriet coldly. "He had a huge lunch before the funeral. Run along, Simon love, you can watch television in the sitting room till all these people have gone."

"Wizard!" shouted Simon and escaped.

Celia moved on into the gathering, and found herself standing next to Clara Winthrop, who did not notice her and seemed to be in a trance. She was staring raptly across the room at a spot where Jack Martindale, in full breeding plumage, was displaying his over-sexed peacock charms to an awestruck blonde.

George Glenville, who had followed Celia across the room, touched Clara on the elbow. She started up out of her trance, and she and George exchanged glances which Celia found difficult to interpret. But neither spoke.

Celia passed on, followed by George, and presently ran into Philip and Eve Glenville, George's elder brother and sister-in-law. "Celia!" cried Eve. "How are you? We haven't seen you for ages."

Philip Glenville was staring over her shoulder at his brother. "Hi there, George, how are you?" he called. But George ignored him and moved away sharply. Celia remembered that the two had quarrelled. But George seemed to be not on speaking terms with Philip rather than vice versa.

She was shocked by Philip's appearance. He was not looking well, and his hair, once a brilliant auburn, had gone sandy-grey and very thin. He had been making a slow recovery from a serious operation, that was why she had not been in contact with him and Eve for some time. But he claimed to be full of energy and anxious to see her. "Eve, fix something," he demanded.

"How about lunch next Sunday?" said Eve.

Celia accepted, and they exchanged news till another couple joined them. "See you on Sunday, Celia," Philip called after her as she slipped away.

She went over to a table set out with food and drink, and found that she was standing next to Susan Winthrop. "Where's Ronald?" she asked.

"Over there," said Susan with an impish grin.

Even in his best suit, Ron was alluringly muscular. He was in conversation with Clara. Or rather, he was being talked to by Clara with an energy which amounted almost to sexual harrassment.

"You know she's a closet nymphomaniac, don't you?" Susan murmured.

114

Celia left as soon as she decently could. She had an appointment she was not looking forward to with Inspector Bagshaw, and she wanted to get it over as soon as possible.

After a reminder from regional headquarters which Bagshaw knew he must not ignore, he had reluctantly telephoned Mrs Grant at Archerscroft and asked her to meet him after the funeral at the police station in Beckley. She made difficulties about this, but he turned down her alternative proposal of a rendezvous in a pub. He would not demean himself. There was to be no cosy get-together over a drink, but a formal interview in his office, with him asking the questions.

His appointment with the crystal-gazing prophetess from Welstead had prompted a good deal of ribaldry among his colleagues, which he had not discouraged. A surprising number of them found they had business to do in the more public parts of the building as she passed through them on the way to his office. What they saw was a tiny, slim figure which could have been that of a child, an enormous pair of dark glasses, a nose and a tightly wrapped headscarf. There was quite a lot of sniggering behind her back.

In the privacy of Bagshaw's office she began removing her disguise. "That's better," he commented acidly. "Not a pop star, are you?"

What was revealed was good features, silver-grey hair and an icy, ladylike poise as Celia, rigid with indignation at being gaped at and mocked by the whole of Beckley CID, waited for him to open the conversation.

He was still convinced of Harding's guilt, but Parker's rival theory seemed to him an excellent theme with which to put her in her place. "Friend of the family, aren't you? Tell me a bit about them, can you? Lady Clandon, now. A bit nervous, isn't she?"

"Well, she has to look after a great estate and bring up the heir to it. The prospect must be pretty daunting."

"Jumpy when you ask her questions, I meant."

"I haven't asked her any, so I don't know," she replied, wondering what he was getting at. Did he know that Harriet had lied about the key?

I thought as much, useless as a witness, Bagshaw decided. Too close to the family. And his question had touched a raw nerve. She was holding something back.

"The countess and Mr Glenville. Good friends, are they?"

"It's a purely business relationship, I think, because he manages the estate. On the personal level, she dislikes him."

"Any particular reason?"

She thought. "He's very efficient, but has a rather aggressive way of going about it, and as a person he's ambitious and very cold. He can also be quite violent. When Harding attacked me, Mr Glenville intervened really viciously, using far more force than the occasion called for."

True or false? Perhaps Glenville was Lady Clandon's lover as Parker suggested, and this fey little piece of goods was covering up for them. He put on the pressure. "You don't like him, Mrs Grant? What makes you think Lady Clandon doesn't?"

"She made several very critical remarks to me about him."

Fey little Mrs Grant could be telling the truth. If the pair were lovers, they had good reason to keep quiet about it and put on an act.

He decided to change the subject. "What are her relations with the local travel agent, Mr Martindale?"

"I don't think she has any, except on the business level. He's widely known to be a promiscuous sex-athlete."

"But I have been told on good authority that he was Lady Clandon's lover before her marriage."

"If that's the case I know nothing about it, Inspector," said Celia coldly.

116

Hear no evil see no evil speak no evil, Bagshaw thought, that's her line where the family's concerned. I shall lose my temper if I don't get her out of my office quick.

"Mr Martindale was at Winthrop early that morning. So Lady Clara says. Fond of her father, I dare say. Would resent it if her stepmother had a lover."

Go on, my dear, he told himself. Take offence, why don't you, and stalk out of the room.

But she had remained icily composed. "As she hated both the men you have mentioned, I wonder what candidate you have in mind? Shall we change the subject? You haven't asked me about Susan Winthrop yet."

"No. Seen a lot of her, formed my own opinion."

Right, thought Celia. Now it's my turn to administer a put-down. "I'm sure you're not foolish enough to think Susan interfered with those plant labels. The murderer wasn't in a position to attack Lord Clandon in the house, and needed to create an opportunity to have a go at him outside. We agree, don't we, that he changed the labels around to get Lord Clandon out into the garden early in the morning, when no one was about?"

Yes, he thought, but there's a snag you silly woman. He started to point this out, but she swept on. "No, don't interrupt, I know what you're going to say. How did the murderer know he wouldn't leave the labels where they were till later in the day, or get one of the gardeners to attend to them? The answer's simple. The fiddling with the labels was a repeat of something that had happened before. The murderer knew how Lord Clandon behaved then, and expected him to do the same thing again. Back in the spring Susan and her young man swung the signposts in the garden round so that the one to the lavatories pointed the wrong way and so on. They went on doing it every night for a week, and every time they went back they had to do it again. If Clandon was putting things right early every morning, and the murderer noticed this, he'd realise that it was a pattern he could arrange to repeat."

"How do you know all this?" Bagshaw asked.

"I asked Susan and she told me."

As she had hoped he was furious. "You *asked* her?" he thundered.

"Yes."

How dare she forestall him? He had worked it out for himself, and had intended to put the same question to Susan when he had time. "Meddling amateurs . . . interfering with the course . . . of justice," he spluttered, incoherent with rage.

She had stood up and was putting on the headscarf.

"Sit down and listen to me," he managed.

"Thank you, I prefer to stand. No, you listen to me. In my time I have met quite a number of policemen as rude and incompetent as you are, who like you disbelieved everything they were told and wasted time barking blindly up all the wrong trees. But never, never up to now have I been summoned to a police station by a yobbo of an inspector in order to be gaped at and sniggered at by the whole CID and turned into a male chauvinist locker room joke. And if Chief Inspector Weaver asks me what happened here, I shall tell him."

She swept out, leaving Bagshaw purple in the face and gasping for breath. Too angry to realise that stress had brought on an acute asthma attack, she swept out of the room and slammed the door.

All along the corridor people emerged from their offices. "Someone had better go in there," she told them. "He seems to be having an apoplectic fit."

More sniggers greeted her passage to the exit. She neither knew nor cared whether they were directed at her or at Bagshaw's discomfiture. Rage soon gave way to relief. She was on Harriet's side now. There were no divided loyalties any more.

118

Chapter Seven

Celia's indignation at Bagshaw's behaviour erupted over Bill when they met for a drink that evening.

"It was obvious the moment I arrived that I'd been built up in advance as a comic turn, the funniest thing the CID there had seen for years. When I got to Bagshaw's office he sat behind his desk twitching that nasty little moustache and taking vicious little nibbles at me with his front teeth like a mad March Hare. Everything he said was an offensive suggestion of some kind, I could murder him."

Bill did his best to calm her down. But she was perplexed as well as angry. Presently she started using him as a testing-ground as she tried to straighten out her ideas.

"He thinks Harriet Clandon has a secret and is 'nervous' in case he unearths it."

"And is she?"

"Anyone in her position would be upset. But she often seems to me tetchy and over-strained, rather than saddened by what fate has dished out to her. That's one of the things that worries me. He also thinks George Glenville is her lover."

"Well Celia, he could be."

"No. Absolutely not."

"You're sure?"

Celia thought about this carefully. "I've a feeling that she finds Glenville physically repulsive, the sort of man she'd rather die than go to bed with. Another woman can often tell about that."

"How about you? Did he turn you off?"

"What repelled me was his violence. He was absolutely brutal to the wretched Harding."

"Why does Bagshaw think he and Lady Clandon got the hots for each other?"

"I think he's probably constructed a nice tidy scenario. Glenville kills Clandon so that they can marry. They then fake a burglary, so that they can collect the insurance."

"Hey Celia, he's crazy. She's loaded, she's got all the Clandon money. Why does he think they want more?"

"I suppose Clandon could have made a very odd will, leaving it all tied up for the little boy, or something. The trouble is, I can't believe they're lovers, none of this fits."

"Could that burglary have been a dodgy fake?"

"There's one thing makes it look genuine. A week or so earlier, there was a security scare, a couple of people disguised as tourists were seen looking around at the wiring and so on, as if they were spying out the land for a break-in."

"Could they have faked that?"

"I shouldn't think so."

"How many people saw them?"

"Let me think. Oh! Yes, you're right. Glenville and Harriet were the only two who saw them doing anything suspicious. One of the guides at the house remembered them, but only when Harriet described them to her and said they were up to no good."

"So there's no proof either way."

"Oh, but there is! They *were* up to no good, they stole a vase!"

"Did they? Or did Lady Clandon hide it somewhere and say it was stolen?"

Celia's spirits slumped. "Oh dear, she could have done. But I still say, none of this fits. They're not lovers. Something's wrong."

"Didn't you say she lied to you? About where she'd put the key to that safe."

"Yes. That was odd. She was being questioned by the police, and she didn't actually speak. When they asked her where she'd put the key she just pointed to one of the drawers. I'd been there the night before when she put it in quite a different one, and I think she hoped I wouldn't see."

"Why did she need to lie about that?"

"Why indeed? That's another thing that doesn't fit. And afterwards, on the way back upstairs, she more or less fainted, as if she'd had a shock. I can't make sense of any of it, can you?"

"No, Celia."

"Oh dear, it gets more complicated every minute. And there's this unbelievable story that one of the Winthrop gardeners told you. About Harriet having had a carry-on with Martindale before she was married, and something about a dirty nightdress."

"Oh Celia, that was only Harry Garton having sex fantasies. He's always on about how the animals go in two by two."

"But Bagshaw's just trotted out a toned-down version of the same story."

"Crikey, has he got sex on the brain too?"

"He has no brain to have sex on," she remarked savagely.

"But he can't have got it from Garton, no one believes a word he says. There must be some such story going round the village."

"Maybe, but it can't possibly be true. As I've said before, Clandon was much too strait-laced to marry a fallen woman, especially one that's been gossiped about."

"And as I've said before, Celia, when it's sex you never know what they'll do."

She looked doubtful. "I still don't believe it, Bagshaw probably dreamed the story up as another offensive suggestion to throw at me."

121

Bill was alarmed to see her getting steamed up again. "Forget him, he's not worth wasting weedkiller on."

"Oh dear, you're right. Answer me this, though. Clara Winthrop says she hates men, but according to her sister Susan she's a nymphomaniac. You've had a lot of them after you, are there nymphomaniacs who hate men?"

"I dunno, Celia. When they come after me, I run a mile."

Next morning Bill loaded up a massive consignment of scarlet pelargoniums, which were to provide the outer band of the Rainbow Bed, and another of vivid green nicotianas for the green band lower down. When he set off for Winthrop, Celia, anxious not to meet Harriet in her present confused state of mind, did not accompany him, but found jobs to do elsewhere.

Garton and Watts were already standing by at Winthrop, ready to begin planting. Garton was displaying a lurid black eye and complaining of aches and pains. Between his groans he went on dispensing his usual flow of scabrous gossip. Kevin's ex-girlfriend had made heroic but vain efforts to rid herself of her unwanted burden by jumping off the kitchen table after drinking enormous quantities of gin. The butcher's wife and the postmistress had indulged in lesbian practices in the lavatories at the village hall. Jack Martindale had been having what looked like very uncomfortable intercourse with the doctor's secretary in the back seat of his small sports car.

Kevin Watts did not believe a word of it. "How would you know about a thing like that?"

"Saw them. Sunday, half-past eleven at night. Happened to go past on me bike."

"Happened to go past where?"

"That picnic place off the lane in King's Wood."

"And what was you doing Sunday night cycling along there?"

Garton winked. "Rabbit snares."

"Martindale see you? Knock you about a bit, did he?"

122

"Nah. Hurt meself last night. Fell downstairs and hit me head on the cupboard. Tell you what, though: I seen Lady Clara with her knickers down and Busyboots Glenville laying into her good and proper."

"Go on," said Kevin.

"Strue. I was up here sixish-sevenish last night to collect me bicycle that I left here. They was in there where the spring roses are, going at it like a two-stroke piston engine on that seat."

"Harry, you bloody liar, I don't believe a word of it. You made it up."

"That's what you think, but you're wrong."

One of the routine duties of Detective Constable Walsh was to pay a daily visit to Peter Harding's house to see if he had surfaced again. After ringing the bell, he always peered into the ground floor rooms, checked the back door and made sure that Harding's car was not back in the garage. On this occasion nothing seemed to have changed, the place was as deserted as ever. But as he was about to leave, the old man who lived in the bungalow opposite came hurrying out to speak to him.

"He's been back."

"Mister Harding has?" Walsh echoed. "He's not there now, and his car isn't in the garage."

"Must have gone off again while we was round the back."

"When did he come then?"

"Last night after we was asleep."

Walsh was puzzled. "How d'you know he's been?"

"I'll show you. Come and look." The old man led the way round Harding's house to the vegetable garden behind it. "I do his garden for him, see?"

Walsh, a family man with a vegetable garden of his own, approved of what he saw. The shallots and lettuces and peas were flourishing in their dead straight rows, the main crop potatoes were well earthed up, and there was not a weed to be seen. The proper rotation of crops was being observed. A broad band in the middle of the plot lay fallow.

The old man halted at the end of it. "I was going to dig that lot over Monday to put in a row or two of leeks for him; he's partial to leeks. But here, see? That bit at the end? He's gone and dug it over hisself."

Walsh looked. There was no doubt that the earth had been freshly disturbed over an area about five feet square. "Does he often dig in the garden?"

"Not him. If he does anything it's the fiddly stuff, snipping at the roses and suchlike."

Walsh drew the necessary conclusions, resigned himself to the inevitable and reported the facts to Bagshaw. As he foresaw, he was told to spend a sweaty morning digging a large hole among the rows of lettuces and peas. In due course he unearthed a glittering object, swathed in a mass of protective cellophane. He was relieved. When detailed to dig in other people's back gardens, he usually found himself unearthing a nasty smelly deceased.

In due course the Augsburg *dessus de table* was photographed in its hole, then lifted out by men in white overalls, with infinite precautions to preserve any fingerprints left on its wrappings. While it was being loaded into their car to be submitted to forensics in Beckley, Bagshaw and Sergeant Simpson went into puzzled conference.

"What d'you reckon, Alan?" Simpson began.

"Why dump it here?"

"They find they can't sell it, so they hide it while they try for a ransom?"

"But why here?" Bagshaw demanded. "Why not a nice cosy safe deposit?"

"He's got it away from the other six jokers. None of them know he has a hide-out here; they probably know him under another name."

"I still say, why not a safe deposit?"

"Doesn't make sense," Simpson agreed.

Bagshaw brooded, then brightened. "Tell you what. Someone else dumped it, not Harding."

"Oh. How come?"

"Nice old gardener. Tidy rows of veg. Someone else comes and digs here, he hits the roof and tells us. Harding knew that would happen. Whoever dumped it didn't."

He fell silent, thinking. Simpson waited.

"Who? Lady Clandon and gentleman friend? Insurance man snapping at their heels, heavy hints about them working a scam. They get scared and decide to dump their bauble. Where? Harding's under suspicion, do the dirty on him, why not?"

"If it's them," said Simpson, "they don't care if the old man sees the disturbed earth and raises the alarm. The sooner the thing's dug up the better."

But Bagshaw was plunged in gloom. "Have to tell the insurance man we've found it, and where. Nuisance. He'll bay at those two like a bloodhound on heat, scare them into fits. No getting any sense out of them after that."

Simpson was alarmed by his superior's change of front. "Are you saying they're guilty and Harding's innocent? With two dozen highly trained operatives tailing his contacts night and day?"

"He's not innocent. He skipped just after Clandon's murder. He fits in somewhere."

"He killed Clandon, but they worked the scam?"

"Could be. That attack on Mrs Grant, when he rocked her car, it must have been drug-related. You'd have to be high on something to do a thing like that."

"He's furious with Clandon for sacking him. So he takes another snort and bashes him with that sledge-hammer thing."

"Having fiddled with the labels on those bushes first? It has to be premeditated."

"Say he's a pusher, and Clandon finds out. That gives us a premeditated killing."

They thought about this.

"Harding links up somehow with Garton, right?" Bagshaw reasoned. "And Garton's got form for drugs."

"So has Ron Fisher. And someone put a load of Ecstasy in that garden temple."

"Any of them could have," said Bagshaw gloomly. "There's been a murder. We'll be round any minute. Panic. They all unload anything they've got, then they're squeaky-clean."

"Why in the garden temple? What's wrong with the toilet?"

"Someone wanted to stitch up Ron Fisher and girlfriend for bashing Clandon."

"The temple's locked. The key was missing. Whoever it was pinched it."

"Garton? He'd be in and out of that estate office. Easy."

"We need to get more on Garton," said Bagshaw thoughtfully. "That gardener chap of Mrs Grant's been working alongside him for days, maybe he's got more sense than she has. Let's have a word with him."

When Bagshaw's call came through, Celia was down in the working area potting on seedlings of *Helleborus corsicus x niger* 'Roger Grant'. Named after her dead husband, it was the first successful cross that Archerscroft had produced, and was still one of their best sellers. Out of superstitious piety she always looked after its propagation herself.

So it was Bill who took the call, which turned out to be for himself. Would he be working at Winthrop next day? He would? Then could Bagshaw have a chat with him somewhere when he knocked off work? Unable to think of an excuse for refusing, Bill agreed and they arranged to meet.

"Your pet hate phoned just now," he told Celia when she was back in the office.

"Bagshaw? Oh horrors. What does he want now?"

"Me. I'm to meet him at the Red Lion in Beckley after work."

"Ha!" exclaimed Celia indignantly.

"Jealous, are you? Because I rate a pint in a pub and you get quizzed in his office without even a coffee."

She ignored this. "What are you going to tell him?"

"What's he going to ask? Ten to one he'll be on about how Kevin Watts said he hated his boss and would like to kill him, and do I know whether he did nor not."

"Did he?"

"No, he's too much of a softie. But he did say he'd like to murder the earl."

"Surely even Bagshaw couldn't take a remark like that seriously? One says that sort of thing. I said I'd like to murder Bagshaw, and I also said I'd like to murder the man who sells us composted bark and gets his accounts wrong. Nobody thinks you mean it."

"Not if you're educated and a lady. If you're an ordinary working man and the police are looking for a murder suspect, it's different."

"Then be careful what you tell him."

"I bloody shall. You'll come over to Winthrop later?"

"No, I'm still in two minds about Harriet Clandon. I'd rather keep out of her way."

"Oh Celia, you got to come. I'll have finished the planting. You must come and inspect, and make sure she's satisfied with the job."

"Bother, you're right, I'll have to. I'll come over about four."

There was plenty to occupy her at Archerscroft, and she spent a busy day divided between the glasshouses and her office. When she arrived at Winthrop, Bill was still planting out the last band of the rainbow, down at the front of the bed.

It consisted of a over a thousand giant pansies in a vivid shade of violet, which Bill had collected that morning on his way to Winthrop. But there had been a delay at the suppliers. "They'd only got eight hundred or so ready for me," he explained. "I'd to pick out the rest from among the mixed colours. That's why I'm not through yet."

While she waited for him to finish the planting, Celia strolled down the garden to judge the effect. It was not nearly as garish as she had feared. Though the bands of colour were well enough defined to make the allusion to a rainbow obvious, there was also just enough foliage to banish any suggestion of tasteless carpet bedding.

On the way back up the slope she wandered off through the specialised rose enclosures. The yellow spring-flowering xanthina hybrids in the first one were getting overblown. But beyond it was an alley flanked with one of her favourites: Nevada, a big shrub rose with single white flowers four or five inches across. The first few buds were opening. But this was one of Lord Clandon's few miscalculations: the alley was too narrow. In another week or so they would be in full June flush, and a visitor would have to fight his way along the alley between arching sprays covered with a cascade of blinding white. Nevada was a spectacular rose to view from a distance, not one to tangle with.

Summoned from the house to admire the finished rainbow bed, Harriet professed herself delighted with it, and decided to have a notice board made to explain that the bed had been planned by her husband shortly before his death, and had been completed in his memory. "We'll put that in the guide books when they're reprinted, and Celia, you will go on keeping it up, won't you?"

Celia agreed hesitantly. She was shocked by the change in Harriet's appearance. Her face was drawn and hollow-eyed and she seemed to be functioning on two levels. While she discussed practical questions with febrile eagerness, half her mind was elsewhere, brooding over some hidden anxiety.

Invited up to the house for a celebratory cup of tea Bill pleaded an engagement, but did not mention that it was with Inspector Bagshaw. Celia too was about to decline, but an imploring look from Harriet made her change her mind. As they walked back together towards the house, Harriet complained again about the behaviour of the loss adjuster employed by her insurers. "So suspicious, he's been treating me as if I was a criminal. But I'm told they all do that now, they get so many fraudulent claims. The other day Lady Forbes said they even looked in the cistern of her loo, in case she'd hidden the diamond brooch in there that she told them she'd lost."

Back at the house, Mrs Holland met them at the entrance to the private wing, looking harassed. "Mr Martindale's here, my lady. I put him in the business room."

Harriet's face froze. "What does he want?"

"To speak to Lady Clara, my lady."

"Oh? Where is she?"

"In the sitting room. She says she won't speak to him, but he says he'll sit there till she does."

Clara was in the window seat of the sitting room, drinking her tea and eating cake. "You'll have to go to him," Harriet told her. "We don't want him sitting there all night."

"I know, but let me finish my tea first," said Clara tetchily.

She took her time over her tea and cake, then rose and went out. "I know what this is about," Harriet murmured. "Jack Martindale wants her to say it was a mistake, she didn't see him in the garden on the morning of the murder."

"Could she have been mistaken?" Celia asked.

"No. She told a deliberate lie."

"Really?"

"Yes. I asked her, and she told me."

"How odd of her," said Celia. "Why?"

"To punish him. She'd given him the thumbs down, but the thought of her millions was too tempting. He went on hanging around here in the hope that she'd change her mind."

"Even so, it seems a bit extreme of her."

"Yes. But you see, she has a built-in hate against men."

"Because her husband got drunk and killed their little girl? That would put anyone off them."

"Except that it was her fault he took to drink. The marriage was on the rocks because she'd been sleeping around."

Celia thought back to her first meeting with Clara, over lunch. "She did say then that she hated men, I remember now. But I thought she was having a dig at her father."

"You're right, she was. She was furious with him. You see, George had had his eye on her millions too. He doesn't have urges about women, I don't think he knows one end of his penis from the other, but he's ambitious and longs to get away from his job here. Unlike Jack, he doesn't have a reputation for fornication on an industrial scale, and that gave him an edge. What with being lonely and depressed, she agreed to marry him."

"Goodness," said Celia. "Wasn't that a bit hasty?"

"Charles thought so. When he found out what was going on he put his foot down, he was a very conventional man. According to him it was indecent, with her husband only three months dead. They must wait at least a year before they married, and there must be no canoodling beforehand to cause scandal. I said there was no point in laying down the law, because if she was made to keep off George she'd only be indecent with someone else, she was made that way. But Charles wouldn't hear of it. It turned out that he didn't want her to marry him at all, I'm not sure why, and thought that if they had to wait a year she'd be bound to jump into someone else's bed and give George the push."

"Goodness. What did Mr Glenville think of all this?"

"Well, he was employed by Charles. He had to do what he was told and keep away from her."

Meanwhile the interview in the business room had overflowed into a noisy shouting match in the corridor.

Then angry footsteps stomped away towards the exit, leaving Clara uttering high-pitched sobs of rage.

"I'd better go and see what's happened," said Harriet, leaving Celia to go home.

During the drive back to Archerscroft Celia wondered why Harriet still gave the impression of bottling up a mass of suppressed anxiety. No scenario she could devise accounted for it satisfactorily. The problem tormented her, but she could see no way through it. In the end she forced herself to think about pleasanter things, mostly horticultural, and arrived back at Archerscroft with a vision in her mind of a narrow path between arching sprays of heart-breakingly beautiful white roses.

Bill's past experience of the police included dealings with an arrogantly wrong-headed inspector who accused him for no obvious reason of murder. This had not endeared the force to him, and he met Bagshaw and Simpson over their pints at the Red Lion in a mood of tight-lipped caution. After attempting a bonding get-together over the fortunes of Southampton football club, Bagshaw got down to business.

"Harry Garton got a bashing the other day. Kevin Watts dish it out to him, did he?"

"Not that I know of. Why would he?"

"Garton had shopped him to me. About the girl he's landed with a bundle."

Bill decided to play this carefully. "Look. Kevin's not very bright, and Harry likes taking the mickey out of people. He tried to throw Kevin into a panic about getting the sack if he didn't marry the girl, and Kevin half-believed it. He did sound off a bit wild, but I talked some sense into him, told him if he got fired because of the girl he could have his lordship's balls off at the tribunal for wrongful dismissal. That was the week before Clandon got his head bashed in, so Kevin had no motive to do it, had he?"

To his relief, Bagshaw explained that he had never considered Kevin Watts a serious murder suspect. "But did he beat up Garton?"

"Why would he?" Bill asked.

"Because Garton told on him."

"I don't think he knew about that. He's a bit soppy really. He must of felt a bit foolish for letting Harry put that scare into him, but he's been acting quite friendly to him since. Kevin's not one to bear a grudge."

Okay, Bagshaw thought. But who, if not Kevin, had given Harry a doing over on the Wednesday evening? He tried a new tack. "Garton's a creepy kind of bloke. Know anything about him?"

"A bit."

"Drug pusher, could he be?"

"No. He's too much of a blabbermouth to keep it quiet. Nothing in his head but drivel about sex."

"Girls he's had, that sort of thing?"

"No, dirty stories about other people's naughty goings-on."

"Kinky," said Bagshaw.

"I think he invents most of it. But Kevin says he's a Peeping Tom, so some of what he says may be for real."

"Tell me some of the things he said."

Bill thought for a moment. "There's a guy called Martindale, that they say has a very itchy groin. Harry said he'd seen this Martindale having it off with a girl, the doctor's secretary I think he said, in a car late one night. And Kevin asked if Martindale saw him spying on them and beat him up."

Bagshaw was suddenly very alert. "Garton say where and when this happened?"

"Yes, in a picnic area in somewhere called King's Wood."

"When?"

"Sunday night."

"You're sure?

132

"That's what he said. Hey, but wait. It couldn't have been then Harry got beat up. He was okay Monday and Tuesday, it was Wednesday he was off work."

Bagshaw's face remained impassive, but his moustache gave a sudden twitch. Nobody but Simpson, who knew him well, would have guessed that he was on to something.

"Next stop Fairsquare Travel and Mr Itchypants Martindale," he said when Bill Wilkins had been thanked and sent home. The travel agency was a few yards along the High Street from the Red Lion. The faded middle-aged blonde in the outer office was no longer grumpy, but greeted them with broad smiles.

"Ah, Inspector, I was hoping you'd call," said Martindale, when she had ushered them into his presence. "Valerie dear, don't go. Inspector, I'd like you to meet Mrs Mason, with whom I have a steady ongoing relationship. Tell him, Valerie dear, what we were doing at the time when I am supposed to have been murdering Lord Clandon."

Valerie admitted happily that her night of love with Martindale, the one just before Lord Clandon's death, had been prolonged until long after Martindale could have risen next morning and killed him.

Martindale beamed at her gratefully. "Thank you, Valerie dear."

Valerie beamed back adoringly, in an aura of new-found sexual prosperity. Clearly Martindale's usual weapon had been deployed to win her loyalty.

Bagshaw made Simpson take solemn notes about where the romance had taken place, but as an alibi it was too unbelievable to be worth checking.

"Will that be all, Inspector?" Martindale asked.

"Not quite. I have been informed that your car was seen in the picnic area in King's Wood late on Sunday night—"

"Valerie dear, you may go," said Martindale hastily.

". . . and that there was a lady with you in it," Bagshaw added as the door closed behind her.

"Well? There's no law against that, is there? Did your informant say who the lady was?"

"Yes, but her identity doesn't concern me."

"Then there's no problem, is there?"

"Except that our informant, who saw what was going on in the car, was badly beaten up three days later."

"Really? I wonder who could have been responsible."

"Someone like yourself who reacted violently against an attempt at blackmail?"

Martindale stared at him hard. "Well, there's no law against that either."

The two detectives drove straight to Winthrop village, and knocked on the door of Garton's cottage. They found him in the middle of what looked like a very unappetising meal in his kitchen. He made a half-hearted pretence of going on eating, but was obviously panicked by their arrival and soon choked on a crumb. When he had recovered a little, Bagshaw waded in mercilessly. "That bashing Wednesday night. It was Martindale, wasn't it?"

"Nah."

"How d'you know it wasn't him? Last time we asked, you said you didn't know who it was."

"Thass right, he had a balaclava on."

"He? Last time you said it was two people."

"Thass right. Two people with balaclavas on."

Bagshaw made a parade of tetchy impatience at such lies, and changed the subject. "Anyone got a grudge against you that you know of?"

"Nah."

"How about Mr Martindale, that you saw doing this and that with a lady in a car, Sunday night?"

"Who told you about that?"

"Never you mind. You did see them, didn't you?"

"I may have gone past there and noticed them. Wass the harm in that?"

"None, but did he see you?"

"Nah."

"But later on he comes and beats you up. How did he know you'd seen them? Because you told him. You asked him for money, didn't you? Said you'd keep quiet about it if he gave you – what? Two hundred? Five?"

"It's a wicked lie, I never," moaned Garton, looking very frightened.

Bagshaw picked up the tobacco tin from the mantelpiece, took out the money and counted it. Five hundred pounds, the sum that had been there on his last visit. "He wouldn't pay up, would he? Gave you a going over and told you to say what you liked, he'd deny it and no one would believe you, because the whole village knows you're an out and out liar."

"You been talking to Martindale. He's the liar, I never said any of that."

"Okay, let's talk about something else." He waved the five hundred pounds under Garton's nose. "Where did this come from?"

Garton looked even more frightened, but said nothing.

"Harding, was it?" Bagshaw demanded. He was convinced that there was a connection between Harding and Garton, and was determined to find out what it was. But the object of this interview was to find out more about Harding, so he decided to adminster soothing syrup to Garton.

"Look, Mr Garton, we're not here to drag you in front of the beak on a charge of blackmail."

He brightened. "You're not?"

"No. We want information from you. Give it us straight, we'll go and you'll be out of trouble."

"Okay. Whass it you want to know?"

"What did Harding get up to worth five hundred quid?"

"Want me to tell on him, do yer?"

"If there's anything to tell."

"Ooh, there is. What I saw when I looked into his bedroom."

135

"Wait. His bedroom's not on the ground floor."

"Nah. I climbed a tree. Round at the back it was. The curtains wasn't properly shut."

"Okay. Who was in the bedroom with him?"

"Reg Smith. The butcher's son that helps in the shop Saturdays."

Garton launched with relish into his description of the scene. Harding was naked. So was the butcher's son, except for a short leather jerkin and a pair of wellingtons. Harding was tied to the bed and the butcher's son was beating him about the back and buttocks with a cane. Discouraged by Bagshaw from providing details of the two participants' physical attributes, Garton came to the point: being only fifteen, the butcher's son was under the legal age for adult games of this kind.

"And you decided that was worth five hundred," said Bagshaw.

"Well it was wicked of him, leading a young lad like that astray."

"And when did you get it off Harding?"

Garton thought. "Six weeks, two months ago."

"But you came back for more, didn't you? And when he saw you were getting greedy he ran away."

The timing of this was important, and Bagshaw phrased his next question carefully. "You put the squeeze on him again, didn't you? When did you ask for more?"

This needed some thought. But Garton worked it out in the end that he had asked Harding for another instalment on the evening before Lord Clandon's murder.

This was not good news to Bagshaw. He broke out into a cold sweat. According to the elderly couple in the bungalow opposite, Harding had fled from his blackmailer early the following morning, before it was generally known that Clandon was dead. So his sudden departure was a coincidence, and nothing to do with the murder. Horrifyingly, the whole case against him had been blown sky high.

That night, Bagshaw had one of the worst asthma attacks of his life. Thanks to him, the regional arts squad had been squandering its scarce resources on an elaborate undercover operation against a group of pathetic, harmless sexual deviants, and in the morning he would have to confess this to Chief Inspector Weaver.

Chapter Eight

Chief Inspector Weaver was bitterly regretting his decision to leave the Winthrop case in Bagshaw's incapable hands instead of taking it over himself. He was not at all amused by Bagshaw's reluctant confession that the alleged gang of country house thieves had turned out to be nothing of the sort. For almost a week, a squad of his highly trained detectives had been trailing round London after a group of deviants whom even the vice squad would have considered beneath its notice.

"I can't see why you're still interested in Harding," he said coldly.

Bagshaw squirmed. In an effort to save face he had decided not to confess that Lady Clandon and George Glenville were now his prime suspects. Instead, he started building up the blackest possible case against Harding. "The stolen object was found buried in his garden," he pointed out, suppressing qualms of conscience. "And he knew where the key to that safe was kept."

"You're saying he's our burglar? As a solo act or with his supporting cast of deviants?"

"By himself. To feed his drug habit."

"He had one, did he?"

"He'd been behaving oddly. Violent too, and full of aggro."

Weaver was not convinced. "Are violent people full of aggro often on the receiving end of fun and games with canes?"

"He half-killed Mrs Grant, sir. Went right over the top.

Clandon sacked him, he had a motive for killing him too. We must find him before he does more damage."

"And how d'you propose to go about that?" said Weaver.

"Round up his contacts, sir, and make them tell me where he is."

No way, Weaver thought. He was not having Bagshaw and his merry men blundering about in the metropolis on Harding's trail. "I think you'd better leave this to us. We'll put the frighteners on these people and make them cough up Harding's London address."

"Oh thank you sir."

But he was not really grateful. He would have preferred to arrest Harding himself, and contrive somehow to maintain an atmosphere of suspicion round him. But there was no help for it, so he rose to go.

Weaver stopped him at the door. "By the way, how did you get on with Mrs Grant?"

"Fine, sir. But I think she'd have told me more if she hadn't been a friend of the family."

Weaver was nervous about having to ask his highly-trained team to concern themselves with such a trivial matter. But they were so amused that he had to call them to order and insist that this was not a joke; there must be no lapse from proper standards of planning and execution. If the deviants were questioned one after the other they would be able to contact each other. Someone would warn Harding that the police were after him. Unless the interviews were synchronised, nothing would be discovered but an empty house or flat. "The idea is to pick them up as they leave their places of work for home," he explained. "Let's forget about the two labourers, they're the rough trade brought in to tickle up Harding and his pals with canes. Go for the respectable ones with a reputation to lose. Which are the married men?"

The chartered accountant, the dentist and the company director were married. "The dentist does an evening surgery," someone objected. "He doesn't leave for home till eight. Want us to march in there and make him leave the patient with his mouth wide open?"

Weaver vetoed this. The interviewees were not to be exposed to public embarrassment. When they had told what they knew about Harding, and a squad car had gone to his address, they could go home and give their families whatever excuse they liked for being late.

One of the detectives volunteered that the bank clerk lived at home with his mother, and therefore as easily pressurised as a married dentist. "Okay," said Weaver and allocated a pair of detectives to each interviewee. "Off you go, then."

The chartered accountant worked in South Kensington and lived in Croydon. The two detectives closed in on him on his way to the underground and showed their credentials. Invited to join them in an unmarked police car for a chat, he said in a frightened falsetto: "Why? I haven't done anything."

"Quite so, sir. We don't intend to accuse you of any offence. All we want is to ask you a few questions about another person . . . No, sir, I can see you're thinking of running away. Please don't. We're both younger and faster than you, it would only cause you public embarrassment."

Plumped down between the two detectives in the back seat of the police car, he shook his head violently when asked if he knew a man called Harding.

"Then perhaps you recognise this photograph, sir."

It was a blown up likeness of Harding, taken from a group photo of the guides at Winthrop.

The unfortunate man trembled violently, hid his face in his hands and groaned.

"Now sir, there's no need to be upset. It's no concern of ours what you get up to in your spare time. We're interested in the man we know as Peter Harding in connection with another matter, and we'd like you to tell us all you know about him."

"Oh. Oh my God!".

"Come on, sir, pull yourself together. Here, take this telephone. Ring your wife and say you've met a client and won't be home till later. Then we'll have a little talk."

The bank clerk, a gangling young man with wispy blond hair, tried to bluster it out. "You've no right to question me like this. My sexual orientation is my own affair."

"Of course it is, sir, no one questions that. What we want to know is, do you or do you not recognise this photo?"

"I've told you. I've never seen the fellow in my life."

"In that case, we'd better go home with you, and see if your mother can throw any light on the matter."

The young man gazed at them in horror.

"Come on now, it won't do you any harm. Tell us what we want to know and you can go home to mum."

The company director, so called, lived in a small terrace house in the grottier end of Wandsworth, with a dirty brass plate on the door alleging something to do with import and export. When the two detectives announced themselves, he had to be dissuaded from escaping down an alleyway at the back of the house. Captured and confronted with the photo of Harding, he let out a gasp of relief. "Oh is that all!"

The detectives had already established that he had two other matters on his conscience. His wife did a thriving trade as a prostitute, and the import-export business, though not prosperous enough to suggest a possible drug connection, was run on somewhat fraudulent lines.

"I like a little tickle on the bottom from time to time," he confessed cheerfully. "What d'you want to know?"

Without the slightest hesitation he told Detective Sergeant Wilcox that Peter Harding in Winthrop was Eric Foster in London, and had a flat in Earls Court. While

Wilcox and his team-mate Fred Jardine drove there to pick up Harding, the others discovered what they could about his background. But it was a mean harvest. Apparently he invited the afficionados to the flat in twos and threes, but the proceedings there were confined strictly to the business in hand, with no socialising before or afterwards. Consequently no one knew anything about their host's family or business connections, though they knew that he spent a lot of time out of London. None of them had been in contact with him in the previous fortnight.

The Earls Court flat was in an Edwardian mansion block. There was no reply to Eric Foster's entryphone and the caretaker had not seen him for a week or two. His mail box in the hall was overflowing with circulars.

The caretaker had a pass key, and had no objection to letting the detectives into the flat. The door was opened but there was no sign of life inside.

But grim death was there, announcing itself by its unmistakable smell.

Harding was in bed, in his pyjamas. An empty whisky bottle and a medicine bottle which had contained Nembutal tablets were on the bedside table beside him. Nothing suggested foul play. He had been dead for a week or ten days at least.

The caretaker bolted in horror, looking queasy. Wilcox telephoned for the proper people to be sent for, and for the interviewees to be allowed to go home. Jardine explored the flat. A large cupboard, presumably containing the apparatus of deviancy, was locked. But on the table in the living room was a notebook, with entries which he began to read.

"What's that, a suicide note?" Wilcox asked.

"No, too long," Jardine reported. "There are pages of it."

The first few pages contained a mass of jottings, entered at different times to judge from the writing. They were religious in tone, mixed up with psychological jargon, which became steadily more incoherent and paranoid as the entries progressed. Two names began to appear at intervals in the jumble of words: Jekyll and Hyde. Presently there was a page with nothing on it but the words 'Jekyll and Hyde, Jekyll and Hyde' written over and over again.

"There was a story about those two," said Wilcox. "Or rather they were one person with two personalities or something. One of them was when he was a goodie, and the other was when he had a letch to make a pig of himself."

"Which was which?" Jardine asked.

"I'm damned if I can remember."

The next few pages made it clear that Jekyll belonged in a place called Winthrop, where there lived a 'pure, wise lady', and that Hyde, who was 'filthy', belonged in London. Eventually this crystallised out into another catch-phrase, repeated right down the page: 'Filthy Hyde in London, pure Jekyll at Winthrop with pure wise Harriet.'

"Harriet must have been his wife," Wilcox decided.

More ramblings followed, in which the words 'filth' and 'guilt' were prominent.

"Hey, what's this?" Wilcox exclaimed as the flipped through the notebook.

Written across two pages in enormous capitals were the words '*FILTHY HYDE WENT TO WINTHROP! HORROR!! GUILT!!!*'

This was repeated over two more pages. Then came one blotched with tears. On it was written in small neat writing: '*When Hyde got to Winthrop it was the end for Jekyll.*'

"The coroner will need this," said Wilcox. "Suicide while the balance of his mind was disturbed, eh?"

"Poor bastard," said Jardine. "No wonder he did it. I would if my mind was as disturbed as that."

*   *   *

143

Saturdays were always busy at Archerscroft, particularly in early summer, and this had been a very busy one indeed. For most of the day the frame yard had been full of customers, some knowledgeable, but others status seekers in search of some rarity which would put their less sophisticated gardening neighbours in their place. Anxious to avoid disappointments which would damage the firm's goodwill, Celia and Bill had been kept busy dissuading the inexperienced from rash purchases which would wither and die within weeks if given the wrong treatment. By evening the cash registers were full and they were exhausted.

Dog-tired, Celia went to bed early and slept heavily till she woke in the small hours from a frightening dream. She was being smothered in something soft and threatening and white, and in the end she realised that it was the Nevada roses. They were attacking her with their arching sprays as she struggled along that too-narrow path at Winthrop. Harriet was calling her from the far end, she had to get through. But the beautiful, sinister rose bushes with their enormous white flowers were tearing at her clothes, forcing her to a standstill. She woke in a cold sweat.

For a long time she lay awake thinking. The vision of the path between the Nevadas had haunted her as she drove home from Winthrop, and glimpses of it had flashed across her mind several times since. Now the huge white roses had turned up as symbols of horror in a terrifying dream. Why?

For a time she dozed miserably, waking at intervals to worry at the puzzle again. Then, just before dawn, she remembered: there was something mysterious about the origins of Nevada.

Wondering why this had not occurred to her hours ago, she slipped on her dressing gown and went downstairs to check with the reference books. Nevada, she found, had been bred and introduced in 1927. According to its breeder it was the result of a cross between *Rosa*

144

moyesii and a hybrid tea called 'La Giralda' which had long since disappeared from circulation. But there was some doubt about its parentage. The geneticists were convinced that the breeder had got his facts wrong. Nevada was a tetraploid, with four sets of chromosomes. *Rosa moyesii* could not have fathered it, because it was a hexaploid, with six. Various people hd suggested that the pollen parent could have been *R. moyesii fargesii* or *R. spinosissima*, both of which had the right chromosome count. But no one knew for certain what the male parent was. Nevada had failed the horticultural equivalent of a blood test.

She crept back into bed, shivering in the chill of dawn, but could not sleep. A train of thought had started and refused to stop. Within half an hour she was up again, ranging along her bookshelves. It took her some time to find what she was looking for: a book on genetics. It was years out of date, but, surely it would give a rough guide? Opening it at the relevant chapter, she read that dark hair, containing a great deal of melanin, tended to dominate genetically over lighter shades, so that the children of one dark-haired parent and a lighter-haired one would tend to have dark hair. As for red hair, 'a special gene works to produce red pigment . . . the degree to which the red shows through depends on the activity of the other hair-colour genes the person carries. When coupled with a gene for black hair, the effects of the red gene will be obscured. But when the red-hair gene is coupled with genes for lighter hair shades, the result may be reddish-gold, chestnut or vividly red hair.'

Even at sixty-five Lord Clandon had been jet-black streaked with grey. According to the book a black-haired person could be carrying the red gene from somewhere among his forebears. She had noticed no red hair among the family portraits at Winthrop. There might have been some hidden under the wigs and pow-dered hair of the eighteenth century, but that was a

145

long way back. So where had Simon's bright red hair come from?

It was fantastic to suppose that Harriet had been an unfaithful wife, but Celia let herself play with the idea for a moment. Jack Martindale was out of the question, he was dark, and anyway Harriet disliked him too much to have anything to do with him. But it came to her in a flash that Philip Glenville, George's elder brother, had been brilliantly auburn before he went grey. And as Harriet and George were both fairish there was not enough melanin around to suppress the red strain which clearly existed in the Glenville family.

It was ridiculous, idiotic, the sort of fantastic idea that should be banished at once. Harriet was repelled by George; it was impossible to imagine them heaving about together in bed, while George's genes asserted themselves and decided that they were to have a red-headed child. On the other hand, perhaps it was not ridiculous at all. In their dealings with Simon they had often behaved like a pair of estranged parents competing for their child's attention in a what the tabloids called a tug of love. Had she once been his mistress, rather than Martindale's? If so, what had happened to make them enemies? Did it have anything to do with whatever had come between George and his elder brother, so that they were not on speaking terms?

Trying in vain to banish these hectic thoughts, she set off to keep her Sunday lunch date with Sir Philip and Lady Glenville at Nosterley. It was a smallish but exquisite Tudor house in rose-coloured brick, with elaborate patterns on the tall chimneys. The diamond-paned windows were large. When it was built England had just become peaceful enough for people to live in houses which were not fortresses. Its only fault from Celia's point of view was its garden, which was fussy without being in period with the house.

Philip and Eve and the tray of drinks were out on the terrace. Philip's illness had stiffened his joints; he

146

had trouble rising to greet her. So far there were no other guests, and as only three basket chairs were in evidence, it seemed that none were expected. For a time they exchanged news of mutual friends. Then a silence fell, and Eve said: "We didn't invite anyone else because we wanted to talk to you about George."

Philip nodded gravely. "You saw how he behaved the other day at Winthrop, making faces and slinking off when I said hullo. I keep trying to bury the damn hatchet, but he won't hear of it."

"We think he's probably unhappy," said Eve. "How well d'you know him?"

"Hardly at all, I'm afraid," Celia replied. "There seems to be a lot of tension between him and Harriet Clandon."

"Oh dear," Philip groaned.

Celia pondered. "Was he working for Clandon before he married Harriet?"

"Yes. When he started there Winthrop was still infested with nuns, and Charley was pigging it in a farm house on the estate. All that grim do-gooding he went in for kept him pretty busy, so he got George in to run the estate for him."

"And then Harriet came along," said Eve. "And of course it was a rather odd marriage."

"Odd? Downright peculiar," Philip agreed. "It must have got well and truly up George's nose. Harriet's turned up trumps in the end, I admire her a lot. But he tends to brood rather on how blue his blood is, and I'm sure he didn't fancy kow-towing to her. As far as he was concerned she was a common little schoolmistress, and everyone knew she'd been bonking with that ass Martindale, who is a sort of public convenience for women."

"I'd heard rumours about that, but did it really happen?" Celia asked.

"Oh yes, didn't you know? I thought everyone did.

147

Martindale was married at the time to a very overpowering lady who was a governor of the village school where Harriet taught, and when she found out what was going on she started to make a very public fuss and the whole village was agog. No one was surprised when Charley Clandon made her pipe down and took Harriet on as his secretary; rescuing fallen women was one of his things. But it was a bit of a facer when he upped and married her a year later."

"He thought he'd sanitised her reputation," said Eve. "But he'd only driven the talk underground. I still don't understand why he did it."

"But you must admit, she was an out and out success as a wife," Philip conceded. "When you're sixty plus, and you've got a super-efficient secretary who's not bad looking and easy to get on with, you marry her and to hell with what people think."

"D'you think that was what got across George Glenville?" Celia asked. "She was efficient and charming and got between him and Clandon?"

"George has a genius for upsetting people," said Eve. "He's always been his own worst enemy."

"Yes, because all the wrong things make him tick," Philip agreed. "He's aways been madly resentful of me being the elder brother with the baronetcy and all the perks that go with it. Even when we were children, he had to keep proving that he could do this and that better than I could. When we were at Cambridge he was so busy being more popular than me that he did no work and got sent down. In the end Father lost patience with him and pushed him into a course on estate management, and that's what he's been doing ever since."

"What brought you and him not be on speaking terms?" Celia asked.

"Oh, he'd been pretty stroppy for years, but the balloon really went up six years ago, just after he started to work for Charley Clandon. What happened was, George applied to the family trust to be given ten thousand pounds to put down as deposit on a house he said he wanted to buy in Winthrop village. It seemed to us perfectly fair; a chap needs a house, so the trustees said okay. But three months later someone else had bought the house, and it soon became clear that the ten thousand pounds wasn't there any more. The trustees threatened to have him on the carpet, but he couldn't face them. Instead, he came and poured out the whole story to me.

"George, you see, had fallen for a scheme to get rich quick. He was dead keen to stop being the younger brother who had to earn his bread and butter, and that made him a bit rash. Unfortunately he still believed something that may once have been true but no longer is, namely that chaps who had been at Eton with you must be as honest as the day. So he listened carefully when one of them, a bloke called Harold Vereker, came to him and said he'd found a picture going dirt cheap that was worth several million; three or four other Etonians were interested in clubbing together to buy it and sell for a huge profit, which they'd share out, so would George like to chip in? According to Vereker the picture had been hanging in a country house up in the north for years, unrecognised for what it was, namely a Van Eyck. He even produced the picture, and a respected authority on the Dutch School, who said it was undoubtedly a Van Eyck, and gave convincing reasons for saying so. The expert was quite right. It was a Van Eyck. But it belonged to a connoisseur who knew perfectly well what it was. Vereker had borrowed it while this chap who owned it was abroad. In due course he put it back where it belonged and vanished to Latin America or somewhere, taking his trusting school friends' money with him.

"Needless to say, I was pretty narked when all this came pouring out, especially when he mentioned that the ten thousand wasn't the only money that he'd thrown down the hole. Apparently the standard stake for taking part in this scam was thirty thousand, and he'd borrowed right left and centre to make up the rest. I said I'd get the trustees to forget about the ten thousand. But I said I was damned if I was going to stump up what he owed to other people, or even lend it to him, whereupon high words passed as they say in novels. So George stomped out of the house, and has never darkened it again."

"But what happened about the money he owed?" Celia asked.

"Ah, that was interesting. A fortnight later, he sent the trustees a cheque for the ten thousand, and surprise surprise, it didn't bounce. And as nobody made him bankrupt, we assume that the other creditors were paid off too."

"Then who came to the rescue?"

"Charley Clandon. It must have been him, there's no one else. I suppose he did it because our father, George's and mine, was Charley's best friend. Even so, it was very unlike him to shell out, he usually came down on sin like a ton of bricks. But you can never tell about people, can you?"

"Was this before or after he married Harriet?"

Philip consulted his wife. "About a year before," said Eve.

Celia thought furiously. Clandon, acting out of character, had put George Glenville under a huge debt of obligation to him. A year later, he had done something even odder for a man of his temperament. He had married Harriet, despite the public disgrace of her affair with Martindale. She too was under an enormous obligation to him. He was devious, secretive and sixty-five years old. To judge from the keen way he had taken Winthrop in hand after Simon was born, he had been longing for years for a male heir.

Philip was saying something to her, and she jerked back to attention. ". . . so you see, being ill like that started me thinking. George isn't a bad chap, and if anything happened to me I'd like my boys to have an older man

150

in the family to turn to, so I'd like to bury the hatchet. Have a go at explaining that to George, would you?"

Celia promised to do so if she got a chance, and they went indoors to lunch. The dining room was darkish, with picture lights over the family portraits hanging on the panelled walls. Ranging round them rapidly before she sat down, Celia found three instances of auburn or red hair. Two of them were in portraits dating from the nineteenth century, to judge from the sitters' clothes. The third was of the First Baronet, in Elizabethan doublet and hose. Auburn hair hung down on either side of his face below his flat silk hat, and his pointed beard was bright red.

Overnight, doubts set in. Plenty of men in their sixties had fathered children, there was no reason why Clandon should have been unable to provide himself with an heir without coercing two people who disliked each other into reluctant adultery. Nor was it at all certain that there was no red hair in the Winthrop genes, or in Harriet's family for that matter. When guided round the house by Harding, she had been too busy with other things to pay proper attention to the pictures.

But she could not let the matter rest. She would check the Winthrop portraits again for any vestige of red hair. If she found any, she would forget the whole thing.

She drove to Winthrop, left her car in the car park used by tourists and put on her headscarf and tinted glasses. Having paid her three pounds for admission to the house, she bought a guide book, and studied it while waiting for the tour to start. It contained a history of the family, from which it became clear that over the centuries there had been quite a lot of intermarriage between the Winthrops and the Glenvilles at Nosterley. According to the family tree on the inside of the cover, two Winthrop daughters had married Glenville sons, and one Glenville daughter had married the eldest Winthrop son. Could she have brought the red hair gene with her to Winthrop?

Evidently not; the young man had died in his twenties, without issue.

This was disappointing. She would have liked very much to dispose of the awkward idea which was bobbing about in her head. It seemed only too probable that Clandon, searching for an heir but unable to produce one, should have turned to a family with close ties, dating back for centuries, with his own. But perhaps she would find a redhead or two in the portraits she was about to see.

The tour started, with a middle-aged woman as guide who was a great improvement on the lovelorn Harding. As they moved along the corridor, she pointed out the best pieces in the wall-cases of Chelsea and Derby porcelain, and was knowledgeable about the furniture and pictures in the state rooms. Unfortunately there were no Elizabethan or Stuart portraits with the sitters exhibiting their own hair, and the bewigged and powdered heads of the eighteenth century told one nothing of the colour underneath. The Regency bucks and their ladies were more revealing, but what they and their Victorian successors revealed was disappointingly dark, and the blonde genes of some of the brides were soon extinguished by the abundant melanin of their husbands.

Then, in the Music Room, there it was, low on the wall. She had missed it last time round, probably because someone tall was standing in front of her. The sitter was a pale-faced woman, with the style of beauty favoured by the painters of the Pre-Raphaelite period. She was tall, with a long neck and, blessed relief, a torrent of red-gold hair.

Celia asked who she was.

"Emily Burkendorf," said the guide, "an American who married the Twelfth Earl. She was lovely, wasn't she?"

The breakfast food heiress, Celia told herself, who had bankrolled Winthrop early in the century.

If the guide had left it at that, all would have been well. But there was a collection of photographs in silver frames on a table under the picture, and among them was a family group portrait: Clandon, Harriet and their son Simon. The guide pointed to it coyly. "That's where the little boy gets his red hair from."

Celia's doubts came surging back. It was of course possible that the picture with Simon in it had been put under the American beauty's portrait as a gimmick, because the tourists were suckers for anything to do with the noble owners and their families. Or was it there because there was a special point to be made: Here is the reason why our son, unlike the rest of the Winthrops for generations back, has red hair?

Had a portrait of a red-haired woman been bought and slipped in among the family pictures to provide Simon with the right genetic credentials? If so, who better to choose for the imposture than his American great-grandmother? According to the family tree in the guide book, Emily, Countess of Clandon had died in 1921. If some American visitor related to her saw the picture, would they know what she had looked like? Or be sure that after her marriage, she had not decided to dramatise her appearance by dyeing her hair?

There was no postcard of Emily among the ones on sale in the entrance hall. This could easily have been simply because there were so many other beautiful things in the house that it had been left out. But it could also be because it ws too dangerous to produce a reproduction of a portrait which was not of the real Emily, in case it was sent to someone in a position to check.

What was she to do? Confront Harriet, she decided and ask for details about the portrait. If she was pefectly relaxed when discussing it, all would be well. If there was any sign of embarrassment, it would be a different matter. Whipping off the headscarf and dark glasses, she went through to the private wing. But Harriet was out. According to Mrs Holland she was doing errands in the village before collecting Simon from playschool.

153

The opportunity was too good to miss. Temptation struck. Stealing was dishonest and against her principles but that could not be helped. Did Mrs Holland think her ladyship would mind if she used the phone to sort out a muddle over an urgently-needed delivery of plants? Of course it would be all right, she could use the one in the business room.

The business room also contained the filing cabinet full of folders of the photos taken for insurance. It was not locked, and folders covering the art objects in the various rooms were there to hand. Uplifting her voice but not the telephone she conducted an imaginary conversation with a supplier of chrysanthemums while she found the folder dealing with the Music Room and stole one of the alleged portraits of Emily from its envelope.

Without waiting for Harriet to return, she drove back to Archerscroft. She knew exactly what to do with the photo. She would send it to Richard Knowles, the authoritative sale-room correspondent of of a leading London daily, whom she had consulted over a previous affair she had been involved in. She posted it off to him with a covering note asking for any information he could give her about it. It was unlikely that he would have any, but she had to try.

Chapter Nine

On balance, Harding's death was a relief to Bagshaw. It was awkward that the confessions in his notebook had more or less demolished the case Bagshaw had built up against him to justify himself to Weaver. But Harding alive and blubbering about his innocence of murder and burglary would have been even more of an embarrassment.

"So we concentrate on Lady Clandon and gentleman friend," Simpson argued. "They're the only starters now Harding's out of the running."

"Is he?" grumbled Bagshaw. "My guts say he is. Can't prove it though."

"Must you prove it?"

"Yes, Chris. Look ahead a bit."

Harding was still an appalling nuisance, even in death. Bagshaw could see himself in the witness box, being grilled by defence counsel for Glenville and Lady Clandon at their trial: "Inspector, why did you arrest this innocent lady and her friend? Isn't it obvious that Lord Clandon was killed by the deceased madman Harding, who had a record of violence and a grudge against the employer who fired him? Don't you agree that you were negligent in failing to investigate this possibility?"

"But look, Alan," Simpson objected. "Harding was insane. The killer was sane enough to fix those plant labels, knowing it would bring Clandon out early, ready to be bashed on the head."

"Insane people are cunning."

"Cunning enough to plant drugs in that garden temple and push off suspicion on to Susan and Ron? There's no talk of drugs in what Harding wrote."

"His scribbles could cover drugs as well as kinky sex," Bagshaw argued.

"And murder?"

"Insane people on drugs do a lot of killing."

"Do they burgle country houses and steal valuable art treasures?"

"They have lucid intervals. They bury the stolen art treasure in their garden."

"But Alan, none of this makes sense."

"Bloody lawyers can make any hogwash sound like sense to a jury. They'd have my balls off if we arrested those two."

"So what next?"

"We know they're guilty. We ferret away till we unearth something."

But the services of a ferret were not called for. That afternoon an enlightening development was handed to them on a plate, and next morning they were speeding up north to interview an elderly couple called Anderson who lived in a village just outside York.

According to the local police they had no criminal record. He was a retired schoolteacher and she was a former nurse.

"Just the sort of people they'd use," Bagshaw commented as they parked in front of the modest semi-detached house in a quiet housing estate. "No form, good background but nothing flashy."

They were being interviewed because the Ripley-based protection organisation for stately home owners had reported a sighting of them at Harewood House near Harrogate. The guides had noted their resemblance to the couple reported to have acted suspiciously at Winthrop.

Their spick and span front room contained an ironing board and some freshly-ironed clothes, a state of affairs which Mrs Anderson considered very shocking and for which she apologised fussily. When these had been removed there was room for everyone to sit down, and the detectives were able to note how completely the couple matched the description of them recorded by witnesses at Winthrop. Mr Anderson was bald, with a fringe of longish hair round the sides and back. His skin was unhealthily yellow, and he had a dark liver blotch on his left cheek. His right leg was stiff and obviously painful to walk on, as had been obvious when he came to open the front door.

The appearance of his wife was less distinctive. She was dumpy, with grey hair, a fattish face and thick glasses, and to judge from the way she peered at the inspector she was very short-sighted. Taken in conjunction with her husband's description, it was good enough to identify her.

"Visited Winthrop Court in Hampshire, didn't you?" Bagshaw began. "On May 24th last."

"We went there sometime in May," said Mrs Anderson. "But I can't remember which day it was."

"It'll be in my diary, Annie," said her husband. "You'd better fetch it."

The diary was fetched, and confirmed that they had indeed been there on 24th May.

Mrs Anderson was surprised. "How did you know?"

"They spotted you at Harewood House last week. Car registration number. Traced you through it."

"I don't understand," stammered Mrs Anderson. "You traced us? Why?"

"Why is he writing all this down?" demanded her husband with an angry glance at Simpson's notebook.

Simpson looked up. "The staff at Winthrop Court reported that you acted suspiciously there. And after you left a valuable vase was found to be missing."

There was a stunned silence.

"You're accusing us of stealing?" asked Anderson in a shocked but furious whisper.

"Only repeating what we've been told. Listen to your answers."

"Our answer, Inspector, is that we totally and utterly reject this filthy accusation."

"Fine, but they say you went into the private wing, tried to get the measure of the security system."

"Nonsense," snapped Anderson. "Why would we want to do that?"

"Spying for a gang of country house thieves."

The old people looked at each other in deep shock. Mrs Anderson was the first to recover her senses. "I know what happened. You remember, don't you Henry dear? You see, Inspector, my husband needed the toilet, and as you see he's very lame. So we asked the man at the ticket desk in the hall if there was one in the house that he could use, instead of having to go all the way round to the ones outside. So we went through a door into the private wing, and a man met us there who said he was sorry there wasn't one on the ground floor, but he'd show us a short way to the one out in the stable yard, so that Henry wouldn't have to go all the way round. He didn't seem to suspect us of anything at the time, but . . . did you say something was missing?"

"Yes," said Bagshaw. "A vase."

"I suppose when they found it was gone, they thought we might have had something to do with it. But we hadn't, really we hadn't."

"So do you withdraw your unpardonable slur on our honesty?" demanded Anderson.

"Not accusing you, only asking questions and getting answers. Travel to Winthrop if necessary, would you?"

"What would be the use of that?" wailed Mrs Anderson.

"Clear the thing up. Could be mistaken identity."

"It damn well is," shouted her husband. "Why should we traipse all over England because you've come here talking malicious nonsense?"

"Information received, we have to check it even if

it's a pack of lies. Pay your expenses to Winthrop, of course."

"I should damn well hope so, Inspector. And now I'll thank you to get out."

As they drove away Simpson said: "I think that clinches it."

"I wish it did."

"But it's just what you said, Alan. Lady Clandon hides the vase, they both say the Andersons acted suspiciously, and after they've faked the burglary they say the Andersons were the reconnaissance party of a country house gang."

"You and I know they're innocent," said Bagshaw bitterly. "Like everything else, we can't prove it."

"So what do we do?"

"See if those two try to brazen it out. If they do, get the old people down to Winthrop to confront them."

When they arrived at Winthrop Court, Glenville was with Lady Clandon in the private sitting room. They faced Bagshaw's questions sitting side by side on the sofa. He explained to them that the Andersons had been traced through the reporting system organised from Ripley.

"Yes," said Glenville. "They phoned to tell us."

Annoyed that they had been forewarned, Bagshaw explained how the Andersons had accounted for their movements.

Glenville shook his head, amused. "They only asked for the lavatory when I caught them poking about in the passage outside the business room. It's the standard excuse."

"They say they didn't steal that vase."

"Well, they would say that, wouldn't they?"

"You think competent spies would give the show away by stealing something?"

"Well, Inspector, there are several possible explanations. They took it because they didn't think they were being paid well enough for their trouble. Or perhaps they

159

didn't steal it, someone else did. Anyway they were definitely spying out the land. They were standing in the stable yard with field glasses, studying the way the wires came into the house. I saw them at it. So did Lady Clandon. Didn't you, Harriet?"

Speaking in a low voice, almost a whisper, she said she had not been present during the Andersons' brush with George Glenville in the private apartments, though she thought she remembered some sort of disturbance in the passage outside her sitting room. Moments later Glenville had summoned her to look out of a window with a view of the yard, and yes, she had seen the two old people standing there, and the man was looking up towards the roof of the house through field glasses.

"And could anyone else have taken the missing vase?"

"I suppose so. But if it had been taken much earlier, one of the guides would have noticed. I think it must have been taken during the tour they were on."

"So that settles that," said Glenville.

"Not quite, sir. Have to bring the Andersons down here, settle the matter once and for all."

The detectives withdrew.

"What now?" Simpson asked.

"We phone that nuisance from the insurance company. Unless we let him in on the act, he'll create like a starving kitten."

Celia was surprised to get a reply so quickly to her query about the portrait of the red-haired American heiress, and disconcerted when she saw the length of the letter from her illustrious sale-room correspondent. Far from knowing nothing about the picture, he did have a great deal to report:

'Dear Mrs Grant,
    Of course I remember you, and with great pleasure. Our association over those stolen Impressionist

160

paintings will deserve a chapter to itself in my memoirs when I get round to writing them.

It so happens that I know something about the picture you are interested in. It was in an auction at Christies' in October 1991, along with a great many competently painted Victorian oils of the sort which even then were ceasing to be unfashionable, though they did not command the enhanced prices the public is prepared to pay for them today. But included in the sale was a group of quite outstanding works by Burne-Jones, Holman Hunt, Rossetti and other members of the Pre-Raphaelite movement. The picture you are interested in was grouped with them in the catalogue because of an apparent resemblance between the sitter and Elizabeth Sidall, the red-haired milliner's assistant who married Rossetti, and served as a model for him, Holman Hunt and most notoriously for John Everett Millais, for whom she lay fully dressed in a tin bath full of water to simulate the dead Ophelia floating down the river amid her garlands of flowers.

The brushwork and general execution of your picture were naive and rather clumsy. It could just possibly have been a very early work by Rossetti, but the authorities mentioned no early portrait by him of Elizabeth Sidall, and another attribution had to be looked for. A label on the back of the stretcher had on it the address of a long-extinct picture framing firm in Darlington, which was known to have been used by an obscure portait painter of the eighteen-eighties operating in the North of England called Arthur John Bilston. This was as near as anyone could get to an identification of the painter, and there is no knowing who the sitter was. She may have been the daughter of some northern manufacturer anxious to display his prosperity and artistic taste as well as his daughter's charms. But Bilston had vaguely Pre-Raphaelite aspirations, and may well have hired a professional model with the right specifications for Pre-Raphaelite beauty, namely striking pallor, a very long neck and a torrent of bright red hair.

Once any association with Rossetti had been discounted, interest in the picture evaporated and it was knocked down to an anonymous purchaser for four hundred pounds. I return your photo herewith and am of course intensely curious to know where the picture is now and what brought it to your notice. If the circumstances are as intriguing as they were last time, I do hope you will confide in me, on the understanding, of course, that nothing will be published till your enquiries are complete.

Yours sincerely,
Richard Knowles.'

Celia wrote him a note of thanks, adding that she could tell him nothing for the present, then sat down to think furiously. What did this discovery prove? Not what she thought at first, in fact her theory was in ruins. The picture had been bought and passed off as a portrait of Emily, Countess of Clandon five years ago. Simon, now the Fifteenth Earl of Clandon, was only four. Therefore it could not have been bought to give a respectable explanation of why his hair was red.

Still wrestling with the implications of this awkward fact, she went across the road to the nursery and tried to carry on with everyday business. But the problem would not go away. She had to give up everything else and concentrate on it. The central fact was that the picture had been bought and passed off as something it was not. There had to be some reason. What was it?

Slowly, the outline of a possible solution began to emerge. It was a horrifying solution, but was it right? That depended on the answer to one simple question which she would have to put to Harriet. She must go to Winthrop and put it to her now. She had to know.

But when she arrived at Winthrop and asked for Harriet, Mrs Holland, looking pale and distraught, said that Her Ladyship was not well. "I don't think she slept all night and she didn't come down for breakfast, and now she's locked herself in her bedroom and won't see anyone."

After thinking for a moment, Celia asked if she could have a word with Lady Clara.

"Of course, madam. She's in the sitting room."

Clara was in her usual seat by the window, absorbed in her book. "Oh, hullo Celia. Something's wrong with Harriet, but we don't know what."

"I think I do."

"Then hadn't you better go and talk to her?"

"I will, but first tell me something. Your little girl, Jessica, who died in the car crash. What colour was her hair?"

Clara frowned. "You sound as if this was important."

"It is. It's part of what's wrong with Harriet. What colour was it?"

"Auburn. The most beautiful red-gold you could possibly imagine. She was such a pretty child. Why d'you want to know?

Celia did not answer. The last piece of the puzzle had fallen into place. She hurried upstairs and knocked on Harriet's door. There was no reaction. The door was locked, so she knocked again. A hoarse voice inside said, "Go away."

"It's Celia. Do let me in. I've something important to tell you."

After a very long pause the bedroom door opened a few inches, and Harriet peered round it in her nightdress. She was was looking ghastly, with dark circles round her eyes.

"My poor Harriet, do let me in. I think I may be able to help."

"You can't." She stood there, holding the door firmly ajar. "No one can."

163

"But I know what's been happening."

"No, you don't know half of it."

"Then tell me, and we'll try to decide what to do."

With a despairing gesture Harriet let her in, ran cross the room and flung herself face down on the bed. "I've told lies, and blackened the name of two perfectly innocent people, and I've got to go on telling lies about them and I hate myself."

Pressed by Celia to explain, she poured out a confused story about a Sevres vase, some people called Anderson and the police. When Celia had sorted this out, it became clear who the Andersons were, that she had been questioned about them, and that Glenville had forced her to lie, threatening dire consequences unless she backed up his version of what had happened. "He said I must tell the police I heard him talking to them in the passage, but I didn't. And I must say I saw them out in the stable yard looking up at the house through field glasses, but that wasn't true. When George called me to the window they were just standing there, but George said I was too late, I'd just missed it, they'd put the glasses away. And that brute Bagshaw says he's going to bring the Andersons here and confront us, and I'll have to tell the same lies all over again."

"Because George Glenville says you must."

"Yes. If I don't he'll tell the world a nasty family secret."

"The secret being that George is Simon's natural father."

Harriet was horror-struck. "You know *that*?"

"Yes. I'm sorry."

Harriet turned over in bed, sat up and looked about her. "Don't be sorry. On thinking it over I'm rather glad to have someone I can talk to about it after all these years." Presently she managed a feverish smile. "Talking about it will be rather a relief. Oh dear, where shall I begin?"

Celia waited.

"You know I blotted my copybook with Jack Martindale before I was married?"

"I'd heard rumours, yes."

"It was awful. I was made to resign from my job at the school because of the scandal, and I was in black misery. But I couldn't move away and start a new life somewhere else because my mother was dying slowly of cancer in our cottage and I had to stay and look after her. So I was enormously grateful to Charles for taking me on as his secretary after the village had written me off as a near-whore, and I did my level best to make myself useful.

"I soon saw that he was miserable. Ever since his first wife died he'd been living in a rather grotty farmhouse on the estate and letting this place to the nuns. He spent his time looking after a mass of charities, which was noble of him but far from amusing, and he had no social life to speak of. The two girls were away from home getting themselves educated and I think he was very lonely. He'd taken a lot of trouble to sanitise me and make Jack's dragon of a wife pipe down about the scandal, and presently he began to be enormously kind to me and treat me more like a daughter than an employee. In the end I grasped that something was brewing, but I was utterly flabbergasted when what was brewing turned out to be a proposal of marriage.

"But when he started to explain the small print of the deal I realised that loneliness wasn't the explanation. Marrying me was part of a devious master plan, and the small print was rather daunting. He told me straight out that I couldn't expect the joys of sex because, unfortunately, old age was taking its toll and his gun was no longer loaded. But he wanted children, and in particular he longed for a male heir to inherit the title. So of course I said what about donors et cetera, to which he replied, no fear. If a lot of doctors and nurses were allowed to fiddle about, too many people

165

would know that the next Earl of Clandon was not his natural child."

What Clandon wanted, Harriet explained, was for her to have a child or children by the son of an old friend of his, descended from a long and honourable line. "And of course it was George I was expected to bed down with. He was already acting as estate manager, and it could all be managed very discreetly because he was living in a cottage attached to the grotty farmhouse. But the whole idea gave me gooseflesh. For one thing, the Martindale business had put me right off sex. Besides, George and I didn't get on. It started when I became Charles' secretary, he thought I was muscling in on his patch and stopping him running the whole place as an ultra-efficient one-man-show.

"I was also worried because men don't keep quiet about their conquests. What would happen if George talked? Charles said he wouldn't because he was under an obligation to him. He owed him a lot of money that he couldn't repay, and as long as he kept quiet Charles wouldn't press him about the debt.

"I was horrified by the idea of becoming a sort of Nell Gwynn, a countess whom everyone knew to be a trollop. On the other hand, the prospect of a quiet life in an isolated farmhouse did seem rather attractive and of course I did owe Charles an enormous debt of gratitude. To do him credit, he never said I ought to do what he wanted after he'd rescued me from the gutter, but I thought about that a lot. Among other things he was paying the nursing home fees for my mother, who didn't die for another year. How could I say no? And what would happen to me if I did? I begged him to think about the donor business again. But he wouldn't hear of it, it was obviously a matter of pride.

"So in the end I said yes, and George and I got down to it. He was a nightmare after Jack Martindale, just a brutal push or two and that was it. He was probably as

166

disgusted with the whole business as I was. At the right time of the month he serviced me coldly as if I was some kind of farm animal, and I had to go through four of these revolting sessions before I managed to conceive. That's why even now, I have to repress a shudder whenever I see George."

"But you must have been overjoyed when Simon arrived," said Celia.

"Yes, and when he turned out to be a boy Charles was over the moon, quite a different person. He had the bit between his teeth, it really frightened me. We were going to turn the nuns out and move back into the big house, and get the furniture and pictures and so on out of store. I was to become an interior decorator and do the rooms up regardless of expense, and he would lay out the garden, and we'd make Winthrop a show place and tourist attraction for Simon to enjoy when he grew up. I was a bit scared, but I've always done what Charles wanted."

"And now he's dead and you're left to pick up the pieces," Celia said.

"Yes, and my God, what pieces! You see, I know now that George pinched that Sevres vase to make it look as if the Andersons were thieves. D'you remember, he tried hard to make Charles let him phone Ripley, so he could give a wrong description and the Andersons would never be traced. He was furious when surprise, surprise the Ripley system disgorged them. I was surprised too, for a different reason."

"But surely, Harriet, you've known all along that he was the burglar? Ever since that night, in fact. You knew the moment you saw what he'd done to the roll-top desk."

She looked up, startled. "How did you work that out?"

"The key to the safe was in one of the small drawers inside the roll-top. I'd seen you put it there the night before the burglary. You knew it was George because he'd broken open two other drawers as well. He was looking for something else."

"Yes. The burglary was a sham, to cover up what he really wanted, the thing in the desk."

"It was a the document about the debt, wasn't it?" said Celia. "The debt that would be called in if he ever spoke out and told the truth about Simon. Did he find it?"

"No. I thought he might try. He'd asked for Charles' keys an hour after he was found dead. That put me on my guard: he'd have gone straight to the desk to take it out and burn it. So I hid it somewhere else, and now he's furious. He's threatening to tell the whole story unless I hand over that wretched piece of paper at once."

"But then he'll have to pay you . . . what was it now? Thirty thousand pounds."

"He was going to say it was a forgery. And he said if I sued him for the money it would only make the stinking scandal worse. Celia, who told you that Charles wasn't really Simon's father?"

Before Celia could answer, a sound made her turn. Clara was standing in the open doorway. "I've been listening outside the door but I couldn't hear properly. May I come in?"

"Of course," said Harriet. "Come and sit by me on the bed. We were just mentioning casually that Charles isn't Simon's biological father."

Clara took this in. "Oh? Then who is?"

"George, believe it or not."

"Good God. He was so bad at it, I was sure he was a virgin. Did you really fancy him?"

"No," said Harriet and explained the circumstances of Simon's conception. "I agree that George is so incompetent he couldn't even have raped the Sabine women satisfactorily, so why are you going to marry him?"

Clara grinned. "He thinks I am, but I'm not."

"Then what was all that fuss with Charles about?"

"You know me, Harriet. I have to have something going

168

on with a man, and the choice round here is pretty limited. So I decided George would have to do, but the moment I started on him the cash register in his head started ringing up my millions and he asked me to marry him. And then one morning Father caught us having a bit of a woo in the garden. He'd have been shocked out of his mind if I'd said George was only a temporary stopgap, so when he told Father he hoped to marry me I had to pretend it was okay by me. All this happened that day when you came to lunch, Celia, and launched the idea of the rainbow bed and everyone said the wrong thing and I managed somehow not to laugh. Just before lunch Father had had a tremendous row with George and we'd both had to promise to behave and keep out of each others' way for at least a year, because I was supposed to be in mourning for my wretch of a husband."

"Charles hoped you'd break it off long before the year was up," said Harriet.

"He didn't just hope," said Celia. "He was determined to stop you marrying, for a very good reason."

She produced the photo of the red-haired beauty from her handbag.

"Where did you get that?" Harriet asked.

"From the filling cabinet of insurance pictures. I'm afraid I stole it."

"It's the American countess from the music room," said Clara. "The one who brought all that money into the family."

"Why were you interested in her?" said Harriet. "I don't understand."

"You see, I have this fatal bump of curiosity. I happened to know that George's brother was red-haired before he went grey, and red hair goes back for generations in the family portraits at Nosterley. Then I wondered why there was only one red-head among the family portraits here, so I made some enquiries about that picture. It isn't the American countess, no one

169

knows who the sitter was. It was in a sale at Christies in 1991, and sold to an anonymous purchaser for four hundred pounds."

"But Celia, I still don't understand," complained Harriet. "That picture was among the things that came out of store when we opened up the big house again."

"Yes. It must have been added to the collection and put in store in 1991, when it was bought."

"So that everyone would think there was red hair in the Winthrop family too?"

"That's right. But did you notice the date? Your husband bought it a year before Simon was born."

"Oh. Then how did he know Simon would have red hair?"

"He didn't. But there was one red-haired child in the family already, and he was afraid there might be another."

"Oh. You mean my Jessica," said Clara.

Harriet frowned. "Now I understand even less."

"I don't think your husband's infertility was just an affliction of old age," Celia explained. "I don't think his gun was loaded when his wife produced Clara and Susan. In fact it never was. This is something that can happen when a boy has mumps in his teens."

"But if Susan and I aren't Father's, whose are we?" demanded Clara. "Not George's, he's only ten years older than me."

"George's father was your father's best friend," Celia explained, "and you are George's half-sister."

It took some minutes for this to sink in. Then Harriet put both hands to her mouth in horror. "Charles was dead against Clara marrying George. George had got his hooks into a woman for the first time in his life. She was rich, and he wanted her money. Charley told him he couldn't have her. Oh my God! He couldn't let her marry her half-brother, could he?"

There was a long silence. Then Clara gave a great cry. "Ugh! men are absolute swine, aren't they?"

170

"I see it all now," said Harriet in a horrified whisper. "Charles gets the famous piece of paper out of the bank to brandish under George's nose, and tells him to lay off Clara."

"Does he say why?"

"I think he has to. Otherwise it looks as if he's being quite irrational and unjust."

"Does anyone else know?" Celia asked.

Harriet thought about this. "No. The whole business of his impotence embarrassed him horribly. He'd never even told me it was a lifelong thing."

"So if Charles was out of the way the secret was safe. I knew in my bones that George had killed my dear Charles, but I couldn't think why. He did it because – oh, how pathetic. He thought, quite wrongly, that with Charles out of the way he could get his hands on Clara's money."

Clara made a choking cry, then dashed into Harriet's bathroom to vomit.

"Poor Clara," wailed Harriet. "Oh Celia, what are we to do?"

"I'm not sure. George mustn't be allowed to get away with this. A murderer who's got away with it once often kills again."

"But how do we stop him?"

Celia concentrated. "Where's the famous piece of paper now?"

Harriet put a finger slily to her nose, and crossed the room to a small gilt and satinwood *bonheur du jour*. A touch on one of the porcelain medallions released a hidden catch. The back of one of the pigeon holes sprung forward and a hidden cavity was disclosed. Harriet pulled out a legal-looking document.

"Risky," Celia commented anxiously. "He might have found it."

"Not really. I told him it was back in the bank."

"What does it actually say?"

Harriet handed it to her. In it George Harold Glenville acknowledged that he had committed a serious fraud, and that out of consideration for his family, Charles Algernon Winthop Earl of Clandon, had agreed to repay the persons defrauded by the aforesaid George Harold Glenville and avoid the scandal of a bankruptcy. To this end he was handing over the sum of thirty-two thousand pounds, to be regarded as an interest free loan, to be repaid by the said George Harold Glenville when circumstances permitted. It was signed by both parties, and witnessed by two clerks in the office of Clandon's solicitors.

"Good,' Celia commented. "If necessary you can produce it, because it doesn't say anything about George being Simon's father."

"If I do produce it, George will say exactly that."

"I think you may have to, if Bagshaw goes on trying to prove that you and George stole the table centre to defraud your insurers."

"I couldn't bear it if George came out with the truth about Simon. I'd feel I was betraying Charley, and goodness knows what the legal position would be."

"Don't worry about that as far as I'm concerned," said Clara, returning pale-faced from the bathroom. "I don't want to be the lady of the manor at Winthrop, and Susan obviously doesn't."

"I don't see how you can stop him speaking out," Celia began, but Harriet interrupted.

"I must! Can't you think of something?"

"There's only one sensible way of handling this," said Celia slowly. "Let him say what he likes, then destroy his credibility so that no one believes him."

"Oh dear. How?"

"Let's invent a scenario. You say that shortly after your marriage, George fell violently in love with you and made determined attempts to seduce you. But you resisted him and told your husband, with the result that there's been bad blood betweed you and George ever

172

since. Nobody Bagshaw asked would say there wasn't bad blood, would they?"

"No."

"Then you say he invented this ridiculous story about Simon to get his own back. Clara then explains that recently George has been making approaches to her, with a view to marrying her and getting hold of her money. But her father opened her eyes to his bad character, and she went off him. Then you produce this document as evidence of his bad character."

"Fine. But why didn't I produce it much earlier?"

"Because you didn't know it existed, or thought it was still in the bank. Yesterday you found it hidden among your husband's vests when you started sorting out his clothes."

"You know, I think this might work," exclaimed Harriet, brightening. "And we can say George thought it was in the desk, and staged the burglary to get it."

"That gets him arrested for burglary, if we're lucky," Clara objected. "But we've no hard evidence that he killed Father, and he ought to get a life sentence for that. D'you think I could get him to confess to murder while we're jolting about uncomfortably in bed?"

"Much too dangerous," said Celia, horrified. "If he spots what you're up to he'll turn nasty and kill you too."

"Then we let him loose on the world to murder other people?" cried Clara indignantly.

"Bagshaw's not stupid," said Celia. "He may come up with something, and after all catching murderers is his responsibility, not yours."

"But meanwhile George has a key to the house and knows the code for the burglar alarm," Harriet remarked with a shiver.

"You can get the code changed," Celia suggested. "Have Susan and her Ron moved back to their flat?"

Harriet made a despairing face. "Yes, unfortunately.

173

Ron's a bit of a bruiser, I'd have been glad to have him around. But the media heat is off them now and they both said they felt uncomfortable amid so much luxury, whatever that means."

"So you two and Mrs Holland will be alone in the house?"

"Yes, unless you agree to join us. Please do, stay and mastermind this tissue of lies we're going to tell."

"I'm sorry, I can't."

"Why not?"

"Because this is the moment when I have to vanish permanently from your life."

"Oh, no!"

"I'm sorry, but if I stay around, the whole thing might blow up in our faces. Richard Knowles, the man who found out about the portrait for me, is a journalist. He's dead keen to get the whole story out of me."

"But you won't tell him?"

"Of course not. But if by some awful chance he found out that I'd been here, he'd be down here like a flash, disguised as a sightseer. And if he saw that picture he'd know at once why I was interested in it, and draw the same conclusions as I did."

"I can take the picture down. Say it needs cleaning or something."

"It's listed in the guide book. Any connection in his mind between me and this house would be very dangerous."

"But must you go now?"

"Yes. Bagshaw will make a move soon, and you'll have to tell your story. The media will make a meal of it, and if I'm in a corner of one of the press pictures Knowles will be on to the story like lightning."

"Oh dear. I thought I had a marvellous new friend. Must you really withdraw from the scene of your triumphs?"

"I'm afraid so, yes. I'm sorry."

"Leaving us at George's mercy."

"Why don't you tell Ron and Susan what's happened? Im sure he'd come back if you asked him and mount guard."

"I might," said Harriet thoughtfully. "What about the Rainbow Bed?"

"It's finished. I'm afraid you'll have to get someone else to maintain it, just in case Knowles makes the connection. We must say goodbye, we really must."

Their farewells were prolonged. Driving out of the stable yard for the last time, Celia was alarmed by the look on Harriet's face, and felt guiltily that she was deserting a sinking ship.

Two days later her morning paper informed her that the ship had indeed sunk, but not in the manner she had expected. George Glenville, the estate manager at Winthrop, had been shot dead by the Countess of Clandon.

Chapter Ten

Nine months later the trial for murder of Harriet Countess of Clandon opened at Winchester Assizes, and at once occupied the front pages of all the tabloids. Even the respectable broadsheets devoted long reports to it. But Celia relied for her information on the local paper in Winchester, for which every day of the trial was a field day.

After the opening formalities, Detective Inspector Bagshaw gave evidence. He said that shortly after one a.m. on the night of 5th-6th June he had been summoned to Winthrop Court, where he found Lady Clandon out in the stable yard beside the house. She was in a hysterical state and claimed that her small son Simon had been kidnapped and was nowhere to be found. After detailing a constable to search the grounds for the child, he had gone into the house and found Lady Clara Williamson, the Countess' stepdaughter, kneeling on an upstairs landing beside a deceased whom he recognised as George Harold Glenville. He had been shot in the chest at close quarters.

Meanwhile the constable searching the grounds had found the child wrapped in a blanket and asleep in a car belonging to the deceased. It was parked some distance from the house, among sheds used for storing lawnmowers and other garden machinery. On learning that the child was safe, Lady Clandon became calmer. He had told her that Mr Glenville was dead, to which she replied: "Oh dear, how awful. I didn't mean to do that."

176

Forensic and other technical evidence took up the rest of the first day. On the second, a barrister representing the insurers of a valuable antique stolen from the house tried to intervene and was given short shrift by the judge.

Lady Clandon then gave evidence. The reporter described her dark blue suit and white blouse, and said that she appeared composed but nervous.

Asked by her counsel to say what had happened on the night in question she replied: "I woke at about one in the morning to find Mr Glenville in my bedroom."

"And what happened then?"

"He told me that he proposed to take my small son Simon away, in other words to kidnap him."

"Did he give any reason for doing so?"

"Yes. He said he would return Simon unharmed provided I handed over a document concerning a debt which he owed to my late husband."

Counsel then asked the clerk of the court to hand the witness a document referred to as Exhibit A, and she identified it as the one in question. It was then passed round the jury, who were asked to note that according to the document, Lord Clandon had lent deceased the money to protect him from bankruptcy: and that in addition to the threat of bankrupty there was a possibility of proceedings for fraud.

Counsel then asked Lady Clandon how she reacted to what the deceased had said. "I ran into Simon's room and saw that he was not in his bed. I couldn't find him anywhere, I was desperate. So I fetched a shotgun and shot Mr Glenville."

"Lady Clandon, was it your intention to kill him?"

"No! I'm not used to firearms, I wasn't brought up in a sporting family. I thought if I hurt him a bit, he wouldn't be able to take Simon away."

"You say you fetched a shotgun. Where did you fetch it from?"

"I had it beside my bed."

"It was loaded?"

"Yes."

"Lady Clandon, why did you keep a loaded shotgun beside your bed?"

"I was frightened of Mr Glenville and what he might do."

"Please tell the court why you were frightened of him."

"He had made one attempt to steal the document, and I was afraid he'd try again."

Asked about the earlier attempt to steal it, Lady Clandon explained that the house had been burgled, ostensibly in order to steal a valuable silver-gilt ornament. But she had been puzzled because locked drawers of her husband's desk had been broken into, although to her knowledge they contained nothing of value. Later, while sorting out her dead husband's effects, she had discovered the document in the pocket of a suit in his wardrobe. She then realised that Mr Glenville was responsible for the apparent burglary. It had been a blind, she said, to cover up the real aim of the break in, namely to get possession of the document. Mr Glenville had broken into the desk because he hoped it was still in there.

Counsel remarked that the pocket of a suit was an odd place to keep a document concerning a debt of over thirty thousand pounds.

"It was in an envelope with markings on it from his bank. This is only guesswork, but I think he must have taken it out to show Mr Glenville, and put it in his pocket because he intended to take it back to the bank. If Mr Glenville saw him lock it in a drawer after showing it to him, it would explain why he broke into the desk."

"Why do you think Lord Clandon took this document out of his bank?"

"Presumably because my husband had just discovered that Mr Glenville wanted to marry my stepdaughter, Lady Clara Williamson. Knowing Mr Glenville's true

178

character, he disapproved strongly. Again, I can only guess, but I think he took the document out of the bank to remind Mr Glenville of his indebtedness, and perhaps threatened to call in the debt if he persisted in his suit."

"Finally, I must ask you again, Lady Clandon, and please think carefully about your answer. Did you intend to kill Mr Glenville?"

"No. I would never willingly kill anyone. And I bitterly regret that I killed Mr Glenville."

That concluded Lady Clandon's evidence in chief and Sir Gordon Fielding for the prosecution, rose to cross-examine her.

"Lady Clandon, did Mr Glenville know the code of your security alarm?"

"Yes. He needed to get into the house in our absence because of his duties as estate manager."

"But you didn't alter the code so that he couldn't get into the house and steal your son. Instead you lay in wait for him with a loaded firearm."

"It's a very sophisticated alarm. The combination can only be changed by a specialist who has to come down from London."

"But you didn't summon this specialist."

"No. I rang the firm twice that day, but they were always engaged. And after that, with so much going on, I forgot to ring them again."

"You . . . forgot."

"Sir Gordon, my husband had been murdered, my house had been burgled, the police and insurance people were everywhere and – yes, I am deeply ashamed to have to confess to you that I forgot."

"So you had recourse to a loaded shotgun to protect yourself. But there is one circumstance which needs explaining. The police found Mr Glenville lying in a pool of blood on the landing outside your bedroom. That is where you shot him?"

"Yes."

"But you say you woke to find him *in* your bedroom."

"Yes. When he told me what he proposed to do I rushed out to look for Simon. He followed me, and waited on the landing."

"I see. And he waited there patiently while you fetched the gun from beside your bed and took it out into the passage to shoot him."

"I pretended I was going to fetch the document he wanted from my husband's dressing-room and give it him."

"But isn't there a telephone by your bed?"

"Yes."

"Why didn't he follow you into the room to prevent you ringing the police?"

"Obviously because he knew I wouldn't, for fear of what he might do to Simon."

"I see. Did you dislike Mr Glenville?"

"I disliked having my son kidnapped."

"I'm sure you understood the meaning of my question. Did you dislike him before the events of that night?"

"He was a very efficient administrator of the estate, but I found him very cold and impersonal."

"Are you sure, Lady Clandon? Was he not a former lover of yours, whom you shot because he had become a nuisance and you were tired of him?"

At this point Lady Clandon appealed to the judge. "My Lord, have I no protection against such insults?"

His lordship replied that counsel was entitled to put to her matters that he thought relevant. Sir Gordon then repeated his question and Lady Clandon replied.

"Mr Glenville and I met almost every day. Our relations were correct but not particularly friendly. No one who saw us together could possibly suspect from our behaviour that we were, or ever had been, lovers."

"You were not disguising your true feelings when you met in public?"

"Certainly not."

"Are you sure? Is it not the case that that Mr Glenville is your son's natural father?"

"Oh really, Sir Gordon! Is there no limit to the filth you propose to throw at me?"

"Unfortunately, Lady Clandon, it is my job to ask questions and yours to answer them, not vice versa. I put it to you that the child is Mr Glenville's son and that you shot him because he was blackmailing you about the matter."

"I find it impossible to imagine how such an absurd suspicion could have entered anyone's head."

"Perhaps because your son takes after Mr Glenville's family, of which several members have red hair."

"Red hair runs in my husband's family too. If you ask Lady Clara, his daughter by his first marriage, she will tell you that her little girl had brilliant auburn hair."

"'Had', Lady Clandon? At what stage did it change colour?"

"Little Jessica was killed, Sir Gordon, in the tragic car accident in which Lady Clara's husband died. But I am sure she will be pleased to provide you with colour photographs of her little girl if you want to pursue this line of enquiry any further."

"Oh dear, that was an unfortunate remark of mine, for which I apologise. I am sorry to have to put these suggestions to you, but it is my duty to do so in the interests of justice. There is one more matter which I must try to clear up. Was fear for your little boy your only motive for killing Mr Glenville?"

"I had no motive for killing him, and didn't intend to."

"I'm sorry. I should have said, was it your only motive for shooting him?"

"Yes, if you call sheer panic a motive."

"Was it not also in your mind that Mr Glenville had almost certainly murdered your husband?"

"I have no idea who murdered my husband, nor have

the police, as far as I know. I don't see what motive Mr Glenville could have had for killing him."

"To remove an obstacle to his marrying Lady Clara?"

"But he didn't have a cat's chance in hell of marrying her. If you ask her she'll tell you she'd been put right off him by what her father had told her about him."

"He could have killed Lord Clandon to obliterate the debt which was hanging over him."

"You don't have to kill someone before you steal a document from them."

"So you maintain that in shooting Mr Glenville you did not have it in mind that he had killed your husband and deserved to die."

"Sir Gordon, I don't believe in capital punishment, nor do I see myself usurping the functions of a public executioner. And I repeat, I had no intention of killing Mr Glenville."

Sir Gordon had no further questions. After a brief re-examination by her own counsel, Lady Clandon had been replaced in the witness box by her stepdaughter who confirmed various statements made by her. Cross-examined by Sir Gordon Fielding she admitted that at at one time she had been very much attracted by Mr Glenville. Sir Gordon asked if she had been in love with him.

"If you wish to put it like that, yes."

"In fact you were having an affair with him."

"Yes."

"Yet a few words from your father were enough to change your mind about Mr Glenville and end your relationship with him."

"What I learned about him was a tremendous shock."

"I see. Where were you when Lady Clandon shot him?"

"I was standing at the other end of the landing."

"But you made no attempt to prevent the shooting?"

"I think I shouted something when I saw what was

going to happen. Then I ran forward to take the gun from her, but it was too late."

"Were you aware that Lady Clandon had a loaded shotgun beside her bed?"

"Yes."

"Did you have one beside your bed?"

"No."

"Lady Clara, I believe your late husband owned a shoot in Yorkshire before you moved to the United States. Are you accustomed to using sporting guns?"

"I have done so, yes."

"Would it not have been better if you had had the gun by your bedside, rather than your stepmother, who had never fired one?"

"Possibly, but I didn't think there was the remotest chance of her needing to use it. She wanted it there to give her reassurance after the upsetting events of the previous few days."

On the following day counsel for the prosecution and the defence then addressed the jury, and made the kind of remarks which might be expected of them. Summing up, the judge reminded them that Lady Clandon had not pleaded self-defence as the justification for her action. She and her advisers had been right not to do so, because shooting someone to prevent them from kidnapping one's child was not, strictly speaking, an act of self-defence. The jury must decide whether they believed Lady Clandon when she said she did not intend to kill Mr Glenville when she fired at him. If they did, it was open to them to bring in a verdict of manslaughter. If they did not, the correct verdict was murder. Since the defendant had admitted firing the fatal shot, these were the only two verdicts open to them.

The jury retired, and emerged three hours later to return a verdict of manslaughter, with a strong recommendation to mercy. The judge, while taking note of their recommendation, said that a person with a grievance, however justifiable, was not entitled to take the law into her own hands. Death had resulted from her act, and it had to be punished. He therefore sentenced Lady Clandon to two year's imprisonment.

Celia saw at once that the whole trial had a subtext. Sir Gordon, on seeing that Harriet had her wits about her, had made offensive suggestions for her to rebut, thus ensuring that the jury would come down firmly on her side and return a verdict of manslaughter. The sentence had to be prison to discourage others from following Harriet's example. In a climate of proliferating crime too many exasperated householders were shooting at burglars instead of doing their civic duty by waiting for the police to arrive hours after the event and fail to arrest them. With remission, the sentence would in practice mean eighteen months at most. It could not be suspended. Harriet could not be seen to be receiving lenient treatment because of her title.

The true events of that night, Celia was sure, had followed a scenario of Harriet's devising. Clara had lured George into the house with a promise of sex. When he arrived it was she, not Harriet who had shot him expertly from a distance of three or four yards. Between them they had wiped the gun clean, then made sure that Harriet's fingerprints were under Clara's, whose prints were on it to establish that she had taken the gun from Harriet to prevent further violence. Harriet had then taken the sleeping Simon from his bed and carried him out into the stable yard. Not finding George's car there must have been a worry, but in the end she realised that he had left it a little distance away to avoid rousing the household. Having deposited Simon in it, she was all ready to present Bagshaw with a picture of a distracted heroine going mad out of doors in her nightdress. She had, in fact, got away literally with murder.

Celia tried very hard to feel shocked. She was a firm opponent of capital punishment, mainly because she was

184

haunted by the knowledge that in one well-known case at least, a man had been hanged who was later found to be innocent. But in this case there was possibility of a mistake. The man Harriet had killed was a murderer, and deserved to die.

Charles Clandon was the only person who knew the truth about Clara's parentage apart from George himself. So he had decided that with Clandon out of the way he could still marry his half-sister and get his hands on her millions. Greed had blinded him to the fact that she had no intention of marrying him. By a stroke of tragic irony, he had committed a completely pointless murder. But there was no way of proving his guilt, and a murderer who had got away with it once was liable to strike again. Knowing this, Harriet and Clara had conspired to put him out of action.

In a furtive telephone conversation with Harriet while she was on bail, Celia had checked that the picture of the unknown redhead had been burnt, and that all mention of it had been deleted from a reprinted version of the guide book. But Richard Knowles, furious because she refused to let him in on the true story of the picture, was employing all the techniques of investigative journalism against her. Any connection between her and Winthrop would expose Harriet to fresh danger, because he would make the connection at once between the picture and the mention at the trial of Simon's red hair.

Shortly after the verdict Philip Glenville telephoned her. Simon was living with him and Eve while Harriet served her sentence, and he had agreed to act as stand-in manager of the Winthrop estate. But neither he nor Eve knew the first thing about gardening. Would Celia take over supervision of the garden at Winthrop till Harriet got back?

This was clearly out of the question. Philip had to be told the truth, but not at Nosterley. She arranged to meet him at a remote country pub, and made sure she had not been followed there. "Philip, have you told anyone you wanted me to look after the garden at Winthrop?"

"I don't think so."

"Well, don't."

"Oh? Why not?"

Celia told him. When he had heard the full story, he said: "Oh lord, I knew George was a bad lot, but this is a new twist. One doesn't exactly relish having a murderer in the family."

"Nobody knows he was a murderer, thanks to Harriet."

"True. One has to hand it to her, I didn't realise she had the guts."

"And the intelligence," Celia added.

"Yes. It was clever of her to leave the actual shooting to Clara, who could bring down a brace of partridges with a right and left when she was fifteen."

"Is Clara still at Winthrop?

"No. She's decided that Frenchmen are better at it, and bought herself a huge house in Versailles. Tell you what though, Celia. There's one good thing come out of this nasty murky business. The ties between Nosterley and Winthrop go back for generations, and it gives me the hell of a kick to know that the Earl of Clandon is my nephew and under my roof. Let's hope he turns out better than his father."

Endnote: Readers interested in genetics may like to know that Celia Grant's reference on page 145 was from Amram Scheinlfelds's *Heredity In Humans*, Chatto and Windus, 1972.